5
1
29
57
74-75
82
88
90
30

Monsieur Teste

new york: ALFRED · A · KNOPF 1947

PAUL VALÉRY

*translated from the French and with a
note on Valéry by* JACKSON MATHEWS

MONSIEUR

THIS IS A BORZOI BOOK,

PUBLISHED BY ALFRED A. KNOPF, INC.

FIRST AMERICAN EDITION

a note on Valéry

Paul Valéry's death in July 1945 had the same *occasional necessity* as the events of his life. It may be said in strict seriousness that he died at the right moment. France, with almost nothing left but her language — reduced, it would seem, to her essential glory — was in sad need of a hero. The moment and the need produced . . . the death of Valéry. His funeral, to the surprise of all outsiders, and with sudden, almost unintended ceremony and splendor, became an occasion of national mourning. All sorts of public honors (election to the French Academy, to a chair at the Collège de France) had made of this modest man, "poet of the intelligence," writer of difficult and illuminating little essays, somehow the official literary figure of his country, despite his protest that he was not really a man of letters at all. And I believe we shall see, when the impossible confusion through which he lived has been turned into a more possible past, that the figure of Paul Valéry stands for his age, as Voltaire and Hugo stand for theirs. As hero and symbol of the mind he is of their stature and, even in his symbolic death, *illustrates* the only France of his time.

Valéry was a southerner, meaning in France

a note on Valéry

a Mediterranean man. His Italian mother and Corsican
father lived on the quay-side at Sète, where he was born in
1871. Until he was grown he had hardly been out of ear-shot
of the Mediterranean, and from that sea his sensibility absorbed the images and energies that stocked his memory: the
harbor at Sète, the noise of dock machinery, the fishing boats,
and the bed of bright fish-entrails under the green surface
near the wharf; the old park at Montpellier darkened with
Poësque cypress trees; the aquarium at Monaco; the steep
streets of Genoa, where he spent his vacations, and the powerful water he drenched himself in all summer. The old cemetery
overlooking the sea at Sète, where Valéry is buried, became
in his mature imagination a great poem.

At school, boredom drove the boy's interests
to architecture, poetry, mathematics, music, painting. He
read Poe's *Eureka*, the poems of Mallarmé, and studied mathematics and Wagner's music with passion. A chance meeting
with Pierre Louÿs at Montpellier in 1890 brought him Paris,
André Gide, and the decisive personal influence of his life,
Stéphane Mallarmé.

Mallarmé's work had given Valéry a peculiar
formative shock. These marvelous little "crystal systems,"
as he called Mallarmé's poems, struck the terror of perfection
into him. Reading them, he could feel nothing but despair
("beauty is that which makes us despair"). He was himself
already writing some very good poems indeed, but now his
mind was driven past poems themselves to wonder how these
"crystal systems" were constructed; the one thing superior
to a perfect poem, he thought, would be a full knowledge of
how it was made. He was soon to give up writing poems himself and turn his intense powers to the study of "the prepara-

tion of these beauties," the generation of poems in the poet's mind. Valéry was already coming into possession of his own and proper subject: *the mind behind the work.*

His decision to renounce poetry was very much like a conversion. The crisis came at Genoa, on a stormy night in August 1892: "A frightful night . . . my room brilliant with lightning . . . and my whole fate being played out in my head . . . between me and me." He decided to leave Montpellier for Paris, where he put up in a student hotel near the Luxembourg Gardens. His room was like a monk's cell, one picture (of a skeleton), and a blackboard always covered with mathematical equations. He was a favorite at Mallarmé's Tuesday evenings.

Giving up poetry was by no means a simple matter. Valéry had for some time felt in literature and art certain serious inadequacies. They did not satisfy the range of his demands to know himself and the world; as method they were too vague, as instruments they were not precise. He was powerfully drawn to mathematics and the exact sciences, to the possibilities of precision, the means of discovery he saw in many branches of knowledge. His rejection of poetry was thus a manner of freeing his mind of an exclusive preoccupation, a manner of clearing his head for the application of new intellectual methods — an acquisition of freedom. Already the range of his interests, the erudition he turned into resources of wit, the serious meanings at play in his gaiety and personal charm, astonished and fascinated the young poets and *littérateurs* who were his friends.

But his new freedom was not easy. Valéry now felt in himself the conflict between several visions of the world demanding to be reconciled. He admired Mallarmé's solution: to make of poetry a metaphysics — conscious control of the poetic processes carried to the point of heroism. In Poe's *Eureka* he found, to our surprise in America, one of the century's great efforts to solve the conflict by turning scientific vision into poetry. But it was in Leonardo that Valéry found the great instance of the whole mind, the mind that had mastered all the arts and sciences, turning them all into instruments of his power. This resolution of an old conflict furnished the theme of the best of Valéry's early prose, in particular two pieces he never ceased to meditate on the rest of his life: *An Evening with M. Teste* (1894), and his *Introduction to the Method of Leonardo da Vinci* (1894–5).

   The death of Mallarmé in 1898 struck Valéry a paralyzing blow. Whether this was the cause or not, the fact is that he now abandoned writing altogether and entered a period of study and inner cultivation of his powers that was to last for nearly twenty years. It was during this part of his life that he developed the habits of work that were so much an expression of his mind: the practice of rising at five in the morning to take notes on the coming of consciousness. For more than forty years this man was up before day, and after a cup of warmed-over coffee, was at his desk noting every nuance of the double dawn staining his window and himself. The notebooks he filled in this way with drawings, meditations, figures, water-colors, scraps and scribblings from the whole life of a great mind at work, now fill the bookshelves of his former study. Their publication, difficult certainly, may yet discover an intellectual mine.

   Valéry returned to the practice of poetry at the insistence of André Gide during the first World War. His first "exercise," as he called it, elaborated over a period of

a note on Valéry

several years and finally published in 1917, took fame by a "poetic *coup d'état.*" This was *La Jeune Parque.* Within the next five years he added the small body of perfect poems that made him the most authentic poet living. "Of all the poets, in any language, of the last thirty years," said T. S. Eliot recently, ". . . it is he who will remain for posterity the representative poet, the symbol of the poet, of the first half of the twentieth century — not Yeats, not Rilke, not anyone else."

Valéry saw everything from the point of view of the intelligence: *tout par rapport à l'intelligence.* The mind, so often said to be his *subject,* might better be called the controlling metaphor of his work, for like all great subjects this one led into the whole world. If Valéry's preoccupation was the pursuit of consciousness, no one knew better than he that the pursuit began in himself, and led through man, the world, and history. "How long will it take us," says Léon-Paul Fargue, "to see that Valéry spoke of just those things men own in common, the least fragile of things: the sky, the sea, beauty, change and the moveless, the taste for solving enigmas, and the great art of being wary of what is called the new." Yet, whatever Valéry was discussing, whether it was Greek geometry, Europe, myth, Descartes, or poetry, his deep concern was always with some maneuver, some possibility, method, or situation (often tragic) of the mind. He looked at seashells, studied mathematical physics, went to a ballet, read Poe, or waked early in the morning, all to the same end, to get the light from these diverse angles, times, and objects upon his obsessive center: the conscious mind.
Consciousness is naturally dramatic, since it

is always embodied, embedded, in its opposite. It is just that quality which cannot be isolated or known. That elusive humanity in us, our Self, is unknowable, said Valéry, because it is "that which knows," it is that generalized awareness which includes, *comprehends*, all we know. It is the irreducible active voice of man. Like the wind, it can be *seen* only in other things. The circle of consciousness closes around its universe of events; all *things* are subordinate to "that pure universality, that insurmountable generality consciousness feels itself to be."

In a beautiful passage of his *Note and Digression* on Leonardo, Valéry turned the dramatic nature of consciousness into this extended figure: Consciousness, he says, is like "*an audience, invisible in the darkness of a theater. A presence that can never see itself, condemned to watch the opposite spectacle on the stage; and yet it knows it fills all that breathing, unalterably oriented night. Complete, impenetrable night, absolute night; but numbered, most avid, and secretly organized night, structured of organisms that limit and press on each other; night compacted of a darkness alive with organs that can applaud or hiss, or be excited, each keeping its place and function, according to its nature. And opposite, facing this intense and mysterious audience, shining, moving in a closed frame, are all Sensible, all Intelligible, all Possible Things. Nothing can be born, die, or be at all, or occupy a moment of time, a place, a meaning, an image — except on this limited stage, circumscribed by destiny, lifted from some primordial chaos as light was separated from darkness on the first day, set off and forever subject to the condition of* BEING SEEN. . . ."

It is this point of view of the intelligence that determines the structure of Valéry's work. It has been said

a note on Valéry

that his *Introduction to the Method of Leonardo da Vinci* is rather an introduction to his own method; for what he did, instead of analyzing the works of Leonardo, was to *imagine at length the structure and operation of a mind* so complete, so universal, that all the sciences, all the arts, were its tools. Then, he said, if such a figure ever actually existed, it was certainly Leonardo. Likewise, in *La Jeune Parque*, whatever may be the difficulties or obscurities of that major poem, whatever its beauties or philosophical import, its subject, as Valéry liked to tease his critics by remarking, was simply *the thoughts of a young girl one night.* Even in his essays on contemporary affairs, it was *the plight of the mind* faced with the facts of modern history that interested Valéry. The mind as it works, loves, knows, suffers in man, lives in science, myth, the arts, or becomes Europe, "brain of the earth's body"; consciousness as it ranges from the lower limits of bodily death or sleep through stages of waking and knowing to the extreme limits of judgment; every gesture, every inter-mediate throe, spark, or step of the mind as it rises from the rich muck of the unconscious to the complex structures of the artistic or mathematical imagination; the human and his-torical condition of consciousness, the *drama of consciousness*, that is the subject of all Valéry's work. He called it the Intellectual Comedy. It was no doubt impossible, in 1894, to feel the full weight of his plain, emphatic announcement: *Intérieurement il y a un drame.*

Monsieur Teste * is, in a sense, Valéry's novel. Teste himself, on the one hand, is an ordinary fictional char-

---

* *Old form of French* tête, *meaning "head"; also from Latin* testis, *meaning "witness," "spectator," and "testicle."*

a note on Valéry

acter, someone anyone might know, the lonely figure of modern city life, a problem in everyday human relations. On the other, he is a mind behaving as a man, or, to put it the other way, "a man regulated by his own powers of thought." *Monsieur Teste* is the story of consciousness and its effort to push *being* off the stage, to use it up. "The character of man," said Valéry, "is consciousness; and the character of consciousness is to consume, perpetually, . . . *the man of mind* must finally reduce himself knowingly to an endless refusal *to be* anything whatever." But is it possible for man to be all mind? Is M. Teste possible? If not, *why is he impossible?* That question, Valéry says, is the *soul* of M. Teste. He is impossible because . . . (shall I presume to answer, in straight prose?) because consciousness cannot entirely consume being and still continue to exist. It depends on being. Sensibility is its home, knowledge is its profession; that is why Valéry had to invent Mme Teste (all soul and sensibility) and Teste's friend (his knowledge of the world).

The pieces that make up the present volume, then, are the occasional results of a lifetime of meditation on the question: *How would a complete mind behave as an everyday man?* It is amazing how much we see of Teste in so few pages; in each part, a different view of him: his author's, his wife's, his young friend's, his own. We see him at the café, the theater, at home, even in bed; we watch him think, make love, sleep, stroll in the park; we witness a vivid re-creation of his milieu, the Paris that contained him; and in his logbook, "the sacrifice of his thought."

Some readers find the logbook an anticlimax. Led to expect so much of this extraordinary man, it is natural that they should find his actual thought not so extraordinary

a note on Valéry

after all. If this little book were to be held strictly to laws of fiction this would have to be counted one of its flaws; but actually, anticlimax is here calculated and necessary, for it reinforces just that impression of the ordinary, the everyday, which is a large part of Valéry's theme: the mind's involvement in daily modes of existence. In the end, the effect makes one of his main points, that it is always "a sacrifice of thought" to write it down; the very act of writing stops thought by making it dependent on words for its expression. M. Teste's logbook is no exception.

The legend identifying M. Teste with Valéry himself has naturally grown up, and has already made perhaps too much of the autobiographical aspects of the work. This is a very personal book indeed, but Valéry was probably no more M. Teste than he was Leonardo, Mallarmé, or Descartes; he was all of these in his own way. Teste is simply the most persistent image of that unknown man, his author's consciousness. He remains, said Valéry toward the end of his life, "the most satisfactory being I have met . . . the only person who endures in my mind."

This note has not aimed to "explain" *Monsieur Teste*. It has served if it shows the way to the text. Valéry in his own preface warns us that his work is not for the lazy reader. His mind was so intense it could not move without saying something; he demands close reading. If you grant him that, his text lights up at once, and you find a style extremely simple and clear. The wonderful resources of rhetoric he manages to draw from such homely clarity make the quality of his style (and make it no doubt impossible to render justly in translation). Yet, Valéry's meaning is never off somewhere in vague spaces of spoofing or speculation, it is in his words. Whatever else he may mean, he always means what he says.

JACKSON MATHEWS

Paris, January 1947

contents:

Monsieur Teste

This imaginary character, whose author I became in my partly literary, partly wayward or . . . inward
youth, has lived, it seems, since that faded time, with a certain
life — with which his reticences more than his avowals have
induced a few readers to endow him.

Teste was created — in a room where Auguste
Comte spent his early years — at a moment when I was drunk with
my own will, and subject to strange excesses of insight into myself.

I was affected with the acute malady of precision.
I was straining toward the extreme of the reckless desire to understand, seeking in myself the critical limits of my powers of
attention.

I was doing what I could in this way to increase
a little the duration of a few thoughts. Everything that came easy
was indifferent and almost offensive to me. The sense of effort
seemed to me the thing to be sought, and I did not value happy
results which are no more than the natural fruits of our native
powers. That is to say, results in general, and consequently
works, were much less important to me than the energy of the
workman — the substance of things he hopes to make. This
proves that theology occurs nearly everywhere.

Monsieur Teste

I was suspicious of literature, even of the fairly precise demands of work in poetry. The act of writing always requires a certain "sacrifice of the intellect." It is quite clear, for instance, that the conditions of literary reading do not allow for an excessive precision of language. The intellect would readily exact of ordinary language certain perfections and purities that are not in its power. But rare are the readers who find pleasure only when their minds are tense. We get their attention only by offering a bit of amusement; and this kind of attention is passive.

I thought it unworthy, moreover, to divide my ambition between the effort to produce an effect on others, and the passion to know and acknowledge myself just as I was, without omissions, pretenses, or indulgence.

I put away not only Literature but nearly all of Philosophy as well among those Vague Things and Impure Things which I rejected with all my heart. The traditional objects of speculation stirred me so little that I thought something was wrong, with philosophers or with me. I had not yet learned that the loftiest problems hardly press themselves upon us, and that they get much of their prestige and their attraction from certain conventions which we must know and accept if we are to be received by philosophers. Youth is a time when conventions are, and must be, ill understood; either blindly rejected or blindly obeyed. It is impossible to conceive, at the beginning of the reflective life, that only arbitrary decisions enable man to found anything at all: language, societies, knowledge, works of art. As for me, I could so little conceive it, that I made it a rule secretly to hold as null or contemptible all opinions and habits of mind which grow out of life in common, out of our external rela-

Preface

tions with other men, and which disappear in voluntary solitude. I could think only with disgust of all ideas and feelings that are induced or roused in man only by his ills and fears, his hopes and terrors, and not freely as when he purely looks at things and into himself.

I was thus trying to reduce myself to my real qualities. I had little confidence in my means, and found within me, with no trouble at all, all I needed to despise myself, but I was strong in my infinite desire for clarity, in my contempt for convictions and idols, in my distaste for facility, and in the sense of my limitations. I had made myself an inner island, and spent my time exploring and fortifying it.

M. Teste was born one day of a memory, then recent, of those moods.

It is in this that he resembles me, much as a child resembles a father who at the moment of conceiving him was himself undergoing a profound change of being, and was not himself.

Perhaps from time to time we do thrust into life the exceptional creature of an exceptional moment. It is not impossible, after all, that the singularity of certain men, the qualities of their difference, good or bad, may sometimes be due to the momentary condition of their begetters. It may be that the transitory is thus transmitted and given career. Moreover, is this not, in matters of the mind, just the function of our works, the act of talent, the very object of our labor, and in short, the essence of that strange instinct to make our rarest finds survive us.

Coming back to M. Teste, and observing that the existence of a creature of this kind could hardly be prolonged into the real much above an hour, I say that the very problem of his existence, and of its duration, is sufficient to give him a kind of life. This problem is a germ. A germ is a living thing, but some germs are incapable of growth. These latter attempt *to live, become deformed, and die. In fact, we know them only by this* remarkable property *of being unable to endure.* Abnormal *are those beings which have a little less future than the* normal. *They are like many of our thoughts, that contain hidden contradictions. Such thoughts occur to the mind, seem just and fertile, but their consequences ruin them, and their very presence is soon deadly to themselves.*

Who knows but that most of the prodigious ideas over which so many great men, and a multitude of lesser ones, have for centuries turned gray, may be psychological deformities — Monster Ideas *— spawned by the naïve exercise of our questioning faculties, which we carelessly apply here and there — without realizing that we should reasonably question only what can in fact give us an answer?*

But the monsters of flesh rapidly perish. Yet not without having existed for a while. Nothing is more instructive than to meditate on their destiny.

Why is M. Teste impossible? That question is the soul *of him.* It turns you into M. Teste. *For he is no other than the very demon of possibility. Regard for the sum total of what he can do rules him. He watches himself, he maneuvers, he is unwilling to be maneuvered. He knows only two values, two categories, those of consciousness reduced to its acts:* the possible *and the* impossible. *In this strange head, where philosophy has little credit, where language is always on trial, there is scarcely a thought that is not accompanied by the feeling that it is tentative; there exists hardly more than the anticipation*

Preface

and execution of definite operations. The short, intense life of
this brain is spent in supervising the mechanism by which the
relations of the known and the unknown are established and
organized. It even uses its obscure and transcendent powers
in the obstinate pretense that it is an isolated system in which
the infinite has no part.

To give some idea of such a monster, to portray
his appearance and habits, to sketch at least a Hippogriff, a
Chimera of the mythology of intellect, requires — and therefore
excuses — the use if not the invention of a forced language, at
times energetically abstract. It requires also a tone of familiarity
and even a few traces of that vulgarity or triviality which we
use with ourselves. We are not reserved toward the one who is
in us.

A text subject to these very special conditions is
certainly not easy reading in the original. All the more must it
present to whoever tries to put it into a foreign language almost
insurmountable difficulties. . . . *

* *This preface was published in French with Ronald
Davis's translation of* An Evening with M. Teste, *Paris, 1925.*

1

An evening with M. Teste

Stupidity is not my strong point. I have seen many persons; I have visited several nations; I have taken part in divers enterprises without liking them; I have eaten nearly every day; I have touched women. I now recall several hundred faces, two or three great events, and perhaps the substance of twenty books. I have not retained the best nor the worst of these things. What could stick, did.

This bit of arithmetic spares me surprise at getting old. I could also add up the victorious moments of my mind, and imagine them joined and soldered, composing a *happy* life. . . . But I think I have always been a good judge of myself. I have rarely lost sight of myself; I have detested, and adored myself — and so, we have grown old together.

Often I have supposed that all was over for

me, and I would begin ending with all my strength, anxious to exhaust and clear up some painful situation. This has made me realize that we interpret our own thought too much according to the *expression* of other people's! Since then, the thousands of words that have buzzed in my ears have rarely shaken me with what they were meant to mean. And all those I have myself spoken to others, I could always feel them become distinct from my thought — for they were becoming *invariable*.

If I had gone on as most men do, not only would I have believed myself their superior, but would have seemed so. I have preferred myself. What they call a superior being is one who has deceived himself. To wonder at him, we have to see him — and to be seen, he has to show himself. And he shows me that he has a silly obsession with his own name. Every great man is thus flawed with an error. Every mind considered powerful begins with the fault that makes it known. In exchange for a public fee, it gives the time necessary to make itself knowable, the energy spent in transmitting itself and in preparing the alien satisfaction. It even goes so far as to compare the formless games of glory to the joy of feeling unique — the great private pleasure.

And so I have surmised that the strongest heads, the most sagacious inventors, the most exacting connoisseurs of thought, must be unknown men, misers, who die without giving up their secret. Their existence was revealed to me by just those showy, somewhat less *solid* individuals.

This induction was so easy that I could see it taking shape from one moment to the next. It was only necessary to imagine ordinary great men pure of their first

An evening with M. Teste

error, or to take this error itself as a basis for conceiving a higher degree of consciousness, a fuller sense of the freed mind. Such a simple process opened curious vistas before me, as if I had gone down into the sea. I thought that I perceived there, dimmed by the brilliance of published discoveries, but side by side with the unsung inventions recorded every day by business, fear, boredom, and poverty, *many inner masterpieces*. I amused myself with smothering known history beneath the annals of anonymity.

Here they were, solitary figures, invisible in their limpid lives, but knowing beyond anyone in the world. They seemed in their obscurity twice, three times, many times greater than any celebrated person — they, in their disdain for making known their lucky finds and private achievements. I believe they would have refused to consider themselves as anything but things. . . .

These ideas came to me during October of 93, at those moments of leisure when thought practices simply existing.

I was beginning to think no more about them, when I made the acquaintance of M. Teste. (I am now thinking of the traces a man leaves in the little space through which he moves each day.) Before I knew M. Teste, I was attracted by his rather special manner. I studied his eyes, his clothes, his slightest low word to the waiter at the café where I used to see him. I wondered whether he felt observed. I would turn my eyes quickly away from his, only to catch my own following me. I would pick up the newspapers he had just been reading, and go over in my mind the sober gestures that rose from him; I noticed that no one paid any attention to him.

I had nothing more of this kind to learn when our relations began. I never saw him except at night. Once in a kind of b—; often at the theater. I heard that he lived on modest weekly speculations at the Bourse. He used to take his meals at a small restaurant on the rue Vivienne. Here, he would eat as if he were taking a purgative, with the same rush. From time to time he would go elsewhere and allow himself a fine, leisurely meal.

M. Teste was perhaps forty years old. His speech was extraordinarily rapid, and his voice quiet. Everything about him was fading, his eyes, his hands. His shoulders, however, were military, and his step had a regularity that was amazing. When he spoke he never raised an arm or a finger: he had *killed his puppet*. He did not smile, and said neither hello nor good-by. He seemed not to hear a "How do you do?"

His memory gave me much to think about. Signs that I could judge by led me to imagine in him unequaled intellectual gymnastics. It was not that this faculty in him was excessive — it was rather trained or transformed. These are his own words: "I have not had a book for twenty years. I have burned my papers also. I scribble in the flesh. . . . I can retain what I wish. That is not the difficulty. *It is rather to retain what I shall want tomorrow!* I have tried to invent a mechanical sieve. . . ."

Thinking about it convinced me that M. Teste had managed to discover laws of the mind we know nothing of. Surely he must have devoted years to this research: even more surely, other years, and many more years, had been given to maturing his findings, making them into instincts.

An evening with M. Teste

Discovery is nothing. The difficulty is to acquire what we discover.

The delicate art of duration: time, its distribution and regulation — expending it upon well chosen objects, to give them special nourishment — was one of M. Teste's main preoccupations. He watched for the repetition of certain ideas; he watered them with number. This served to make the application of his conscious studies in the end mechanical. He even sought to sum up this whole effort. He often said: "*Maturare!*" ...

Certainly his singular memory must have retained for him exclusively those impressions which the imagination by itself is powerless to construct. If we imagine an ascent in a balloon, we can, with sagacity and vigor, *produce* many of the probable sensations of an aeronaut; but there will always remain something peculiar to a real ascent, which by contrast with our imagined one shows the value of the methods of an Edmond Teste.

This man had early known the importance of what might be called human *plasticity*. He had tried to find out its limits and its laws. How deeply he must have thought about his own malleability!

In him I sensed feelings that made me shudder, a terrible obstinacy in delirious experience. He was a being absorbed in his own variation, one who becomes his own system, who gives himself up wholly to the frightful discipline of the free mind, and who sets his joys to killing one another, the stronger killing the weaker — the milder, the temporal, the joy of a moment, of an hour just begun, killed by the fundamental — by hope for the fundamental.

And I felt that he was master of his thought:

I write down this absurdity here. The expression of a feeling is always absurd.

M. Teste had no opinions. I believe he could become impassioned at will, and to attain a definite end. What had he done with his personality? How did he regard himself? . . . He never laughed, never a look of unhappiness on his face. He hated melancholy.

He spoke, and one felt oneself confounded with *things* in his mind: one felt withdrawn, mingled with houses, with the grandeurs of space, with the shuffled colors of the street, with street corners. . . . And the most cleverly touching words — the very ones that bring their author closer to us than any other man, those that make us believe the eternal wall between minds is falling — could come to him. He knew wonderfully that they would have moved *anyone else*. He spoke, and without being able to tell precisely the motives or the extent of the proscription, one knew that a large number of words had been banished from his discourse. The ones he used were sometimes so curiously held by his voice or lighted by his phrase that their weight was altered, their value new. Sometimes they would lose all sense, they seemed to serve only to fill an empty place for which the proper term was still in doubt or not provided by the language. I have heard him designate a simple object by a group of abstract words and proper names.

To what he said, there was nothing to reply. He killed polite assent. Conversation was kept going in leaps that were no surprise to him.

If this man had reversed the direction of his inward meditations, if he had turned against the world the regular power of his mind, nothing could have resisted him.

An evening with M. Teste

I am sorry to speak of him as we speak of those we make statues of. I am well aware that between "genius" and him, there is a quantity of weakness. He, so genuine! So new! So free of all trickery and magic, so hard! My own enthusiasm spoils him for me. . . .

How is it possible not to feel enthusiasm for a man who never said anything *vague?* for a man who calmly declared: "In all things I am interested only in the *facility* or *difficulty* of knowing them, of doing them. I give extreme care to measuring the degree of each quality, and to not getting attached to the problem. . . . What do I care for what I know quite well already?"

How is it possible not to be won over to a being whose mind seemed to transform to its own use all that is, a mind that *performed* everything suggested to it. I imagined this mind managing, mixing, making variations, connections, and throughout the whole field of its knowledge able to intercept and shunt, to guide, to freeze this and warm that, to drown, to raise, to name what has no name, to forget what it wished, to put to sleep or to color this and that. . . .

I am grossly simplifying his impenetrable powers. I do not dare say all my object tells me. Logic stops me. But, within me, every time the problem of Teste arises, curious formations appear.

On certain days I can recover him quite clearly. He reappears in my memory, beside me. I breathe the smoke of our cigars, I listen to him, I am wary. Sometimes, in reading a newspaper I encounter his thought, which some event has just justified. And I try again some of those illusory experiments that used to delight me during our evenings together. That is, I imagine him doing what I have not seen him do. What is M. Teste like when he is sick? How does he reason when he is in love! Is it possible for him to be sad? What would he be afraid of? What could make him tremble? . . . I wondered. I kept before me the complete image of this rigorous man, trying to make it answer my questions. . . . But it kept changing.

He loves, he suffers, he is bored. People all imitate themselves. But he must combine in his sigh, in his elemental moan, the rules and forms of his whole mind.

Exactly two years and three months ago this evening, I was at the theater with him, in a box someone had offered us. I have thought about this all day today.

I can still see him standing with the golden column of the Opera; together.

He looked only at the audience. He was *breathing in* the great blast of brilliance, on the edge of the pit. He was red.

An immense copper girl stood between us and a group murmuring beyond the dazzlement. Deep in the haze shone a naked bit of woman, smooth as a pebble. A number of independent fans were breathing over the crowd, dim and clear, that foamed up to the level of the top lights. My eyes spelled a thousand little faces, settled on a sad head, ran along arms, over people, and finally flickered out.

Each one was in his place, freed by a slight movement. I tasted the system of classification, the almost theoretical simplicity of the audience, the social order. I had the delicious sensation that everything breathing in this cube was going to follow its laws, flare up with laughter in

An evening with M. Teste

great circles, be moved in rows, feel as a mass *intimate*, even *unique* things, secret urges, be lifted to the unavowable! I strayed over these layers of men, from level to level, in orbits, fancying that I could join ideally together all those with the same illness, or the same theory, or the same vice. . . . One music moved us all, swelled, and then became quite small.

It disappeared. M. Teste was murmuring: "We are *beautiful*, extraordinary, only to others! *We* are eaten by others!"

The last word stood out in the silence created by the orchestra. Teste drew a deep breath.

His fiery face, glowing with heat and color, his broad shoulders, his dark figure bronzed by the lights, the form of the whole clothed mass of him propped by the heavy column, took hold of me again. He lost not an atom of all that at each moment became perceptible in that grandeur of red and gold.

I watched his skull making acquaintance with the angles of the capital, his right hand refreshing itself among the gilt ornaments; and, in the purple shadow, his large feet. From a distant part of the theater his eyes came back to me; his mouth said: "Discipline is not bad. . . . It is at least a beginning. . . ."

I did not know what to answer. He said in his low quick voice: "Let them enjoy and obey!"

He fixed his eyes for a long time on a young man opposite us, then on a lady, then on a whole group in the higher galleries — overflowing the balcony in five or six burning faces — and then on everybody, the whole theater full as the heavens, ardent, held by the stage which

we could not see. The stupor they were all in showed us
that something or other sublime was going on. We watched
the light dying from all the faces in the audience. And when
it was quite low, when the light no longer shone, there re-
mained only the vast phosphorescence of those thousand
faces. I saw that this twilight made these beings passive.
Their attention and the darkness mounting together formed
a continuous equilibrium. I was myself attentive, *necessarily*,
to all this attention.

M. Teste said: "The supreme simplifies *them*.
I bet they are all thinking, more and more, *toward* the same
thing. They will be equal at the crisis, the common limit.
Besides, the law is not so simple . . . since it does not include
me — and — I am here."

He added: "The lighting is what holds them."
I said, laughing: "You too?"
He replied: "You too."

"What a dramatist you would make," I said
to him. "You seem to be watching some experiment going on
beyond the limits of all the sciences! I would like to see a
theater inspired by your meditations."

He said: "No one meditates."

The applause and the house lights drove us
out. We circled, and went down. The passers-by seemed set
free. M. Teste complained slightly of the midnight coolness.
He alluded to old pains.

As we walked along, almost incoherent phrases
sprang from him. Despite my efforts, I could follow his words
only with great difficulty, finally deciding merely to remember them. The incoherence of speech depends on the one
listening to it. The mind seems to me so made that it cannot

An evening with M. Teste

be incoherent to itself. For that reason I refused to consider Teste as mad. Anyway, I could vaguely make out the thread of his ideas, and I saw no contradiction in them; also, I would have been wary of too simple a solution.

We went through streets quieted by the night, we turned corners, in the void, by instinct finding our way — wider, narrower, wider. His military step subdued mine. . . .

"Yet, *I replied,* how can we escape a music so powerful! And why should we? I find in it a peculiar excitement. Must I reject this? I find in it the illusion of an immense effort, which suddenly might become possible. . . . It gives me *abstract sensations,* delightful images of everything I love — change, movement, mixture, flux, transformation. . . . Will you deny that certain things are anæsthetic? That there are trees that intoxicate us, men that give us strength, girls that paralyze us, skies that stop our speech?"

M. Teste put in, in a rather loud voice:

". . . But, sir, what is the 'talent' of your trees — or of anyone! . . . to me! I am at home in MYSELF, I speak my language, I hate extraordinary things. Only weak minds need them. Believe me literally: *genius* is *easy, divinity* is *easy.* . . . I mean simply — that I know how it is conceived. It is *easy.*

"Long ago — at least twenty years — the least thing out of the ordinary that some other man accomplished was for me a personal defeat. I used to see only ideas stolen from me! What nonsense! . . . Imagine thinking our own image is not indifferent to us! In our imaginary struggles, we treat ourselves *too well* or *too ill! . . .*"

He coughed. He said to himself: "What can a

man do? . . . What can a man do? . . ." He said to me:
"You know a man who knows that he does not know what
he is saying!"

We were at his door. He asked me to come in
and smoke a cigar with him.

On the top floor of the house we went into a
very small "furnished" apartment. I did not see a book.
Nothing indicated the traditional manner of work, at a
table, under a lamp, in the midst of papers and pens.

In the greenish bedroom, smelling of mint,
there was only a candle and, sitting around it, the dull abstract furniture — the bed, the clock, the wardrobe with a
mirror, two armchairs — like rational beings. On the mantel,
a few newspapers, a dozen visiting cards covered with figures,
and a medicine bottle. I have never had a stronger impression
of the *ordinary*. It was *any lodging*, like geometry's *any point*
— and perhaps as useful. My host existed in the most general interior. I thought of the hours he had spent in that
armchair. I was frightened at the infinite drabness possible
in this pure and banal room. I have lived in such rooms. I
have never been able to believe them final, without horror.

M. Teste talked of money. I do not know how
to reproduce his special eloquence: it seemed less precise than
usual. Fatigue, the silence becoming deeper with the late
hour, the bitter cigars, the abandon of night seemed to over-
take him. I can still hear his voice, lowered and slow, making
the flame dance above the single candle that burned between
us, as he recited very large numbers, wearily. Eight hundred
ten million seventy-five thousand five hundred fifty. . . . I
listened to this unheard-of music without following the calculation. He conveyed to me the fever of the Bourse, and

An evening with M. Teste

these long series of names of numbers gripped me like poetry. He correlated news events, industrial phenomena, public taste and the passions, and still more figures, one with another. He was saying: "Gold is, as it were, the mind of society."

Suddenly he stopped. He was in pain.

I again scanned the cold room, the nullity of the furnishings, to keep from looking at him. He took out his little bottle and drank. I got up to go.

"Stay awhile longer," he said. "You don't mind. I am going to get in bed. In a few moments I'll be asleep. You can take the candle to go down."

He undressed quietly. His gaunt body bathed in the covers, and lay still. Then he turned over and plunged farther down in the bed, too short for him.

He smiled and said to me: "I am like a plank. I am floating! . . . I feel an imperceptible rolling under me — an immense movement? I sleep an hour or two at the very most; I adore navigating the night. Often I can not distinguish thought before from sleep. I do not know whether I have slept. It used to be, when I dozed, I thought of all those who had afforded me pleasure; faces, things, minutes. I would summon them so that my thought might be as sweet as possible, easy as the bed. . . . I am old. I can show you that I feel old. . . . You remember! When we are children we *discover* ourselves, we slowly discover the extent of our bodies, we express the particularity of our bodies by a series of efforts, I suppose? We squirm and discover or recover ourselves, and are surprised! We touch a heel, grasp the right foot with the left hand, take a cold foot in a warm palm! . . . Now I know myself by heart. Even my heart. Bah! the world is

all marked off, all the flags are flying over all territories. . . .
My bed remains. I love this stream of sleep and linen: this
linen that stretches and folds, or crumples — runs over me
like sand, when I lie still — curdles around me in sleep. . . .
It is a very complex bit of mechanics. In the direction of the
woof or the warp, a very slight deviation. . . . Ah!"

He was in pain.

"What is it?" I said. "I can . . ."

"Nothing . . . much," he said. "Nothing but
. . . a tenth of a second appearing. . . . Wait. . . . At certain
moments my body is illuminated. . . . It is very curious.
Suddenly I see into myself . . . I can make out the depth of
the layers of my flesh; and I feel zones of pain, rings, poles,
plumes of pain. Do you see these living figures, this geometry
of my suffering? Some of these flashes are exactly like ideas.
They make me understand — from here, to there. . . . And
yet they leave me *uncertain*. Uncertain is not the word. . . .
When *it* is about to appear, I find in myself something confused or diffused. Areas that are . . . hazy, occur in my
being, wide spaces suddenly make their appearance. Then I
choose a question from my memory, any problem at all . . .
and I plunge into it. I count grains of sand . . . and so long
as I can see them . . . My increasing pain forces me to ob-
serve it. I think about it! I only await my cry, and as soon
as I have heard it — the *object*, the terrible *object*, getting
smaller, and still smaller, escapes from my inner sight. . . .

"What is possible, what can a man do? I can
withstand anything — except the suffering of my body, beyond a certain intensity. Yet, that is where I ought to begin.
For, to suffer is to give supreme attention to something, and

An evening with M. Teste

I am somewhat a man of attention. You know, I had foreseen my future illness. I had visualized precisely what everybody now knows. I believe the vision of a manifest portion of
the future should be part of our education. Yes, I foresaw
what is now beginning. At that time, it was just an idea like
any other. So, I was able to follow it."

He grew calm.

He turned over on his side, lowered his eyes;
and after a moment, was talking again. He was beginning to
lose himself. His voice was only a murmur in the pillow. His
reddening hand was already asleep.

He was still saying: "I think, and it doesn't
bother at all. I am alone. How comfortable solitude is! Not
the slightest thing weighs on me. . . . The same reverie here
as in the ship's cabin, the same at the Café Lambert. . . . If
some Bertha's arms take on importance, I am robbed — as
by pain. . . . If anyone says something and doesn't prove it
— he's an enemy. I prefer the sound of the least fact, hap-
pening. I am being and seeing myself, seeing me see myself,
and so forth. . . . Let's think very closely. Bah! you can
fall asleep on any subject. . . . Sleep can continue any
idea. . . ."

He was snoring softly. A little more softly
still, I took the candle, and went out on tiptoe.

2 *Letter from Mme Emilie Teste*

KIND SIR: I send you our thanks for your nice present and for your letter to M. Teste. I can imagine the pineapple and the jam were no disappointment; I am sure the cigarettes pleased him. As for the letter, I should deceive you if I said the slightest thing about it. I read it to my husband, but I can hardly say I understood it. And yet, I confess that I took a certain pleasure in it. I do not mind listening to things that are abstract or too lofty for me; I find an almost musical delight in them. A good part of the soul can enjoy without understanding, and in me it is a large part.

So I read your letter to M. Teste. He listened to it without showing what he thought of it, or even that he was thinking of it. You know he reads almost nothing with his own eyes, which he uses in a strange, as it were *inward*, way. I am mistaken, I mean: a *particular* way. But that is not it at all. I don't know how to express myself; let's say *inward, particular,* and *universal,* all at once!!! His eyes are quite beautiful; I love them because they are a little larger than visible things. No one ever knows whether anything at all escapes them, or indeed, whether, on the other hand, the whole world is not simply one detail in what they see, a *will-o'-the-wisp* that can obsess, but doesn't exist. Never, my dear sir, since I was married to your friend, have I been able to be sure of his eyes. The very object they fix upon is perhaps the very object his mind wants to reduce to absolute nothing.

Our life is still as you know it: mine, dull and useful; his, all habit and absence. It isn't that he doesn't wake up, and reappear, when he wants to, terribly alive. I like him this way. He is tall and dreadful suddenly. The machine of his monotonous acts explodes; his face sparkles; he says things that often I only half understand, but they never fade from my memory. But I mean to hide nothing from you, or almost nothing: *sometimes he is very hard.* I don't think anyone can be as hard as he. He shatters your mind with a word, and then I am like a defective vase the potter throws in the trash. My friend, he is as hard as an angel. He does not realize his strength: he finds unexpected words that are too true, words that destroy people, that waken them in the midst of their stupidity, face-to-face with themselves, quite trapped in what they are, living so naturally on nonsense. We live quite at our ease, each in his own absurdity, like fish in water, and never perceive except by some accident all the stupidity contained in the life of a reasonable person. We never think that what we think con-

Letter from Mme Emilie Teste

ceals from us what we are. I certainly hope, my friend, that we are worth more than all our thoughts, and that our greatest merit before God will be for having tried to settle on something more solid than our mind's babbling to itself, admirable as that may be.

And yet, M. Teste does not need to talk in order to reduce people around him to humility and an almost animal simplicity. His existence seems to nullify all others, and even his whims can make you think.

But don't imagine he is always difficult or overbearing. If you knew, my friend, how otherwise he can be! . . . Certainly, he is hard at times; but at other times, he wears an exquisite and surprising gentleness that seems to fall upon him from heaven. He makes a mysterious and irresistible present of his smile, and his rare tenderness is a winter's rose. Yet, it is impossible to foresee either his kindness or his violence. It is vain to anticipate either harshness or favor from him; his deep abstraction and the impenetrable order of his thoughts baffle all the ordinary calculations human beings make upon the character of their fellows. I never know what my attentions and kindnesses, or my thoughtlessness and little shortcomings will draw from M. Teste. But I confess that nothing endears him to me more than this uncertainty of his humor. After all, I am quite happy not to understand him too well, not to foresee every day, every night, every next moment of my stay on earth. My soul has a greater thirst for surprise than anything else. Expectation, risk, a little doubt, exalt and vivify me much more than possession of the certain. It is probably not good, but I am like that, despite my own reproaches. More than once I have confessed the thought that I preferred to believe in God rather than to see Him in all His glory, and was reprimanded. My confessor told me this was nonsense rather than a sin.

Excuse me for writing you about my poor self, when all you want is to have some news of your friend who interests you so much. But I am somewhat more than a mere witness of his life; I am part and somehow an organ of it, though nonessential. Husband and wife as we are, our actions are composed in marriage, and our temporal necessities pretty well adjusted, in spite of the immense and indefinable difference between our minds. So, I am obliged to speak incidentally of myself in speaking of him. Perhaps it is hard for you to imagine what my situation must be with M. Teste, and how I manage to spend my days in the intimacy of such an unusual man, finding myself at once so near and so far from him?

Women of my age, my real or apparent friends, are quite amazed to see me, a fairly attractive woman, evidently so well suited for a life like theirs, not undeserving of a simple and comprehensible lot, accept a situation they cannot in the least imagine for themselves in the life of such a man, whose reputation for strangeness shocks and horrifies them. They do not realize that the least sign of tenderness in my dear husband is a thousand times more precious than all the caresses of theirs. What is love for them, always the same, always repeating itself, love that has long ago lost everything that partakes of surprise, the unknown, the impossible, everything that charges the slightest touch with meaning, risk, and power, that makes the substance of a voice the soul's only food, and in short makes all things more beautiful, more significant — more luminous or more

Letter from Mme Emilie Teste

sinister — more remarkable or more empty — according to our intuition of what is going on inside an ever-changing person who has become mysteriously essential to us?

You see, one would have to be quite inexperienced in pleasure, to want it unmixed with anxiety. Naïve as I am, I can still imagine how much is lost from the voluptuous pleasures by taming and accommodating them to domestic habit. Surrender and possession which really answer each other, gain infinitely, I believe, by starting from ignorance even of their approach. Their supreme certainty must spring from a supreme uncertainty, and declare itself like the catastrophe of a drama whose course and conduct we could hardly trace, from calm up to the extreme threat of the event. . . .

Fortunately — or not — I am never sure myself of M. Teste's feelings. And to be so matters less to me than you would believe. Strangely married as I am, I am so with my full knowledge. I knew very well that great souls settle down only by accident; or indeed in order to have a warm room where whatever fraction of woman can come into their scheme of life will always be touchable and kept. It is not distasteful to see the sweet shine of a fairly pure shoulder dawn up between two thoughts! . . . Gentlemen are like that, even the deep ones.

I do not mean this for M. Teste. He is so strange. The truth is, nothing can be said of him that is not incorrect at the moment! . . . I think he must have too much sequence in his ideas. He loses you at every turn in a web that he alone knows how to weave, break off, or catch up again. He draws out in himself such fragile threads that only with the help and concert of all his vital powers can they withstand their own tenuity. He stretches them over what private abysses I do not know, and ventures no doubt far from ordinary time into some chasm of difficulties. I wonder what he is like there? It is clear that one is no longer oneself in those straits. Our humanity cannot follow us toward such distant lights. His soul, no doubt, changes into some peculiar plant whose root, rather than whose foliage, grows unnaturally toward the light.

But isn't this extending oneself beyond the world? Will he find life or death, at the extreme end of these expeditions of his attentive will? Will it be God, or some frightful sensation of encountering, at the bottom of thought, only the pale ray of his own miserable matter?

You ought to see him in these excesses of absence! His whole appearance changes — and fades! A little more of this absorption, and I am sure he would become invisible! . . .

But, my friend, when he comes back to me from the depths! He seems to discover me like a new land! I appear before him, unknown, new, and necessary. He seizes me blindly in his arms, as if I were a rock of life and real presence, on which his great incommunicable genius seems to strike and run aground, after so much monstrous and inhuman silence! He falls upon me as if I were the earth itself. He wakes in me, finds himself in me; oh what joy!

His head is heavy upon my face, and to all his nervous strength I am a prey. He has a force and frightful presence in his hands. I feel as if I were in the clutches of a stone-cutter, a doctor, or an assassin, under their brutal and precise handling; and in terror I imagine that I have fallen into the claws of an intellectual eagle. Shall I tell you all my thought? I believe he doesn't know exactly what he is doing, what he is kneading.

His whole being, which a moment ago was concentrated in one *place* on the frontiers of consciousness, has now lost its ideal object, an object that does and does not exist, since it is only a matter of a little more or a little less *intensity*. It took all the energy of a great body to sustain in the mind that diamond instant which is at once the idea and the Thing, both the entrance and the end. Well, sir, when this extraordinary mate captures and in a way masters me, and puts upon me the imprint of his strength, I have the impression of being substituted for that object of his will which he has just lost. I am like the plaything of a mind that is all muscle. (I express myself as best I can.) The truth he was seeking seems to take on my strength and living resistance, and by some quite ineffable transposition, his inner will passes out and is discharged through his hard and determined hands. These are very difficult moments. What can I do at such a time? I take refuge in my heart; and there I love him as I wish.

As to his feeling for me, as to what opinion he may have of me, these are things I do not know, just as I do not know anything else about him except what can be seen and heard. I have already told you my suppositions; but I do not really know what thoughts or schemes he spends so many hours on. I remain on the surface of life; I move with the current of days. I tell myself that I am the servant of that incomprehensible moment which decided my marriage, as if of itself. Wonderful moment, perhaps supernatural?

I cannot say that I am loved. You can

Monsieur Teste

imagine that the word "love," so uncertain in its ordinary meaning and shifting among so many different images, is no longer valid at all in the matter of the relations of my husband's heart to my person. His head is a sealed treasure, and I don't know whether he has a heart. Do I ever know whether he concentrates on me; whether he loves me or studies me? Or whether he studies himself by means of me? You will understand that this is not important. In short, I am aware of being in his hands, among his thoughts, like an object that is sometimes the most familiar, sometimes the strangest thing in the world, according to the mode of his variable vision, as it adapts to me.

If I dared recount to you a frequent impression of mine, just as it comes to me, and as I have often confided it to Father Mosson, I should say, figuratively, that I feel myself living and moving in a cage which his superior mind has closed around me — *simply by existing.* His mind contains my own, as a man's mind contains the child's or the dog's. But let me explain. Sometimes I wander through our house, going and coming; the notion strikes me to sing, and I skip and dance in improvised gaiety and unrequited youth from one room to another. But however wildly I may leap, I never cease to feel the rule of that powerful absent figure, there in some armchair, thinking, smoking, looking thoughtfully at his hand, slowly testing each one of its joints. Never do I feel my soul without bounds. But surrounded, and enclosed. My goodness! How difficult it is to explain. I do not mean at all *captive.* I am free, but classified.

What we have that is most ours, and most precious, is obscure to ourselves, as you know quite well. It seems to me I should lose my being, if I knew myself

Letter from Mme Emilie Teste

completely. Well, to one person I am transparent, I am seen and foreseen, just as I am, without mystery, without shadows, without possible recourse to the unknown in me — to my own ignorance of myself!

I am a fly, flitting away my little life in the universe of an unchanging eye; sometimes seen, sometimes unseen, but never out of sight. I know at every moment that I exist in an attention always vaster and more general than all my vigilance, always quicker than my sudden and quickest thoughts. The greatest impulses of my soul are to him tiny and insignificant events. And yet, I have my own part of the infinite . . . I feel it. I cannot help realizing that it is contained in his, and I cannot consent that it should be so. It is an inexpressible thing, my friend, that I should be able to think and act absolutely as I will, without ever, *ever* managing to think or will anything that is unforeseen, important, or novel to M. Teste! . . . I assure you that such a constant and strange feeling gives me some very deep thoughts. . . . I may say that at every moment my life seems to me a practical model of man's existence in the divine mind. I have personal experience of being in the sphere of another being, as all souls are in Being.

But alas! this very awareness of a presence one cannot escape, the sense of being so intimately foreknown, cannot but lead me sometimes into base thoughts. I am tempted. I tell myself that this man is perhaps damned, that I run great risk in his company, that I am living in the shade of an evil tree.

But I perceive almost at once that these specious reflections themselves contain the hidden danger they warn me to guard against. I sense in their subtle turns a very clever temptation to dream of another and more delicious life, of other men. . . . And I am horrified at myself. I review my lot; I realize that it is as it must be; I tell myself that I *will* my fate, that I choose it anew every moment; I hear within me, clear and deep, the voice of M. Teste calling me. . . . But if you knew by what names!

No other woman in the world is called by such names as I am. You know what ridiculous names lovers give each other: what appellations of puppy and bird are the natural fruit of carnal intimacy. Speech of the heart is childish. The voice of flesh is elemental. M. Teste, moreover, thinks love consists in *the right to be silly beasts together* — the complete license of silliness and bestiality. So he calls me in his own way. He nearly always designates me according to what he wants with me. The name alone he gives me tells me what I am to expect, or what I must do. When it is nothing in particular he wants, he calls me *Being* or *Thing*. And sometimes he calls me *Oasis*, which I like.

But he never tells me I am silly — which touches me very deeply.

Father Mosson, who has a great and kindly curiosity about my husband, and a kind of pitying sympathy for a mind so apart, tells me frankly that M. Teste inspires in him sentiments very difficult to reconcile with one another. He told me the other day: *Your kind husband's faces are innumerable!*

He finds him "a monster of loneliness and curious knowledge," and explains him, although with regret, as a victim of pride, the pride that cuts us off from the living, and not only from the now living but from the eternally living — a pride that would be quite abominable and almost satanic were it not that, in that over-exerted soul, this pride is turned so bitterly against itself, knows itself so minutely, that perhaps the evil in it is somehow denatured at its source.

"*He is frightfully cut off from the good,*" said Father Mosson, "*but he is fortunately cut off from evil. . . . There is in him some frightening purity, some unquestionable detachment, force, and light I do not know. I have never observed such an absence of trouble and doubt in an intelligence so deeply stirred. He is terribly tranquil! No malaise of the soul can be attributed to him, no inner darkness — and nothing, moreover, that derives from the instincts of fear or greed. . . . But also nothing that is directed toward Charity.*

"*His heart is a desert island. The whole extent and energy of his mind surround and defend it; its depths isolate and guard it against the truth. He flatters himself that he is quite alone there. . . . Patience, dear lady. Perhaps, one day, he will find some print upon the sand. . . . What happy and holy terror, what salutary fear, when he shall realize, by that pure vestige of grace, that his island is mysteriously inhabited! . . .*"

Then I told Father Mosson that my husband often reminded me of a *mystic without God. . . .*

"*What a flash!*" said Father, "*What flashes of truth women sometimes derive from the simplicity of their impressions and the uncertainty of their language! . . .*"

But at once, and to himself, he replied:

"*A mystic without God! Luminous nonsense! . . . It's easily said! . . . False light. . . . A mystic without God, madame, why no movement is conceivable without direction and sense, without finally going somewhere! A mystic without God! . . . Why not a Hippogriff, or a Centaur!*"

"Why not a Sphinx, Father?"

He also feels Christian gratitude toward
M. Teste for the freedom allowed me to follow my own faith
and give myself to my devotions. I have full liberty to love
God and serve Him, and can share myself very happily between my Lord and my dear husband. M. Teste sometimes
asks me to tell him about my prayers, to explain as exactly
as I can how I go about them, how I apply and sustain myself in them; and he desires to know whether I really lose
myself in them as I imagine. But hardly have I begun to
search for words in my memory when he anticipates me,
questions himself, and putting himself prodigiously in my
place, tells me such things about my own prayer, giving such
an exact account that it is clarified and in some way overtaken in its highest and most secret reaches — and he reveals
to me its direction and desire! . . . In his language there is
some power I do not know, to make you see and hear what is
most deeply hidden within you. . . . And yet, his are human
words, only human; they are only the very intimate forms of
faith reconstructed by artifice, and marvelously articulated
by a mind incomparable in audacity and depth! It would
seem that he has coldly explored the fervent soul. But in his
reconstruction of my burning heart and its faith, there is a
frightful absence of its very essence which is *hope.* . . . There
is not a grain of hope in M. Teste's whole substance;
and that is why I am somewhat uneasy at this use of his
power.

I haven't very much more to tell you today.
I make no excuse for having written you at such length,
since you asked me to do so and since you say you have an

Letter from Mme Emilie Teste

insatiable appetite for all the deeds and doings of your friend. Yet I must end somewhere. It is now time for our daily walk. I am just going to put on my hat. We shall walk slowly down through the terribly stony and crooked little streets of this old city, which you know slightly. We usually end by going down where you would like to go if you were here, to the ancient park where all the people of thought, care, and monologue go toward evening, as water goes to the river, and gather necessarily together. There are scholars, lovers, old men, the disillusioned, and priests, all *absent* men of every kind. They seem to be seeking mutual loneliness. They must like to see and not know one another, and their separate disillusionments are accustomed to meeting. One drags his illness with him, another is pursued by his anxiety; they are shades running from themselves and each other; but there is no other place to run from others than here, where the same notion of solitude irresistibly draws each of these absorbed beings. In a short while we shall be there in that place worthy of the dead. It is a botanical ruin. We shall be there a little before twilight. You can imagine us, walking with short steps, giving ourselves to the sun, the cypresses, and the cries of birds. The wind is cold in the sun, and the sky, at times too beautiful, oppresses my heart. The hidden cathedral rings out. Here and there are round pools, built up as high as my waist. They are full to the brim with black impenetrable water, on which are fixed the enormous leaves of the Nymphaea Nelumbo; and the drops that venture onto these leaves roll and shine like mercury. M. Teste muses over these large living drops, or perhaps strolls slowly among the "beds" with their green labels, where specimens of the vegetable kingdom are more or less cultivated. He enjoys this rather ridiculous order and delights in spelling the baroque names:

> *Antirrhinum Siculum*
> *Solanum Warscewiezii*!!!

And the *Sisymbriifolium*, what jargon! . . . And the *Vulgare*, and the *Asper*, and the *Palustris*, and the *Sinuata*, and the *Flexuosum*, and the *Præaltum*!!!

"*This is a garden of epithets*," he said the other day, "*a dictionary and cemetery garden. . . .*"

And after a while, he said: "*Learnedly to die. . . . Transiit classificando.*"

Please accept, kind sir, all our thanks and good wishes.

EMILIE TESTE

3

Excerpts from M. Teste's Logbook

A prayer: Lord, I was in the void, infinitely nothing and tranquil. I was disturbed from that state, to be thrown into this strange carnival . . . and you took care that I should be endowed with all I needed in order to suffer, enjoy, understand, and be wrong; but incompatible, these gifts.

I consider you the master of that darkness I look into when I think, and upon which the last thought will be inscribed.

Give me, O Darkness, that supreme thought. . . .

But in general any commonplace thought may be the "supreme thought."

If it were otherwise, if a thought could be *supreme of itself* and *by itself*, we should be able to come on it by reflection or chance; and having found it, we should have to die. This would amount to being able to die of a certain thought, simply because there is no other to follow.

I confess that I have made of my mind an idol, but I have found no other. I have heaped upon it offerings and insults. Not like a thing of mine. But . . .

————

An analogy to de Maistre's remark on the conscience of a gentleman! I do not know what a fool's mind is like, but an intelligent man's is full of foolishness.

————

I do not know a certain thing, cannot grasp a certain thing; but I *know* Portius, who does have a command of it. I have command of my Portius, I control him as a man, and he contains what I do not know.

————

Certain people sense that their senses separate them from the real, from being. This sense in them *infects* their other senses.

What I see blinds me. What I hear deafens me. What I know renders me ignorant. I am ignorant of as much, and in so far, as I know. This brightness before me is a blindfold that covers either a night or a light plus . . . plus what? Here the circle closes, of this strange inversion: knowledge, like a cloud over being; the world shining, like an opaque film on the eye.

Take everything away, that I may see.

————

Excerpts from M. Teste's Logbook

My dear fellow, you are "perfectly uninterest-ing." But your skeleton is not, neither is your liver, nor in itself your brain — nor your stupid look, nor those retarded eyes of yours — and all your ideas. If I could only know the *mechanics* of a fool!

———

I am not made for novels or plays. Their great scenes, rages, passions, and tragic moments, far from stirring me, reach me only as rather dim lights, or as rudimentary situations in which every sort of silliness is let loose, in which being is simplified even to stupidity, and drowns instead of swimming in the circumstances of water.

———

In the newspaper, I never read the story that's being shouted, the event that sets every heart palpitating. Where would they lead me, if not precisely to the very door of these abstract problems in which I am already wholly situated?

———

I am rapid or nothing — a restless and reck-less explorer. Sometimes I get a particularly personal view of myself, one that might be generalized.

These views kill other views that cannot be raised to the general — either for lack of power in the seer, or for some other cause?

The result is a man regulated by his own powers of thought.

———

Monsieur Teste

Man always standing on Cape Thought, straining his eyes toward the bounds of things, or of sight. . . .

It is impossible to receive the "truth" from oneself. When we feel it forming (it is an impression), we form at the same moment *another and unaccustomed self* . . . of which we are proud . . . or jealous. . . . (This is the last word in inner politics.)

Between Self clear and Self cloudy, between Self just and Self guilty, there are old hatreds and old accords, old denials and old supplications.

––––––

A SORT OF PRIVATE PRAYER: "I thank the wrong, the insult that roused me, the pang of which has carried me far beyond its ridiculous cause, giving me also such courage and taste for my thought that in the end my work has benefited from my anger; my search for the laws of myself has profited from the incident."

––––––

Why I love what I love? Why I hate what I hate?

Who would not like to upset the table of his desires and distastes? To change the direction of his impulses?

How can it be that I am at once like a magnetic needle and like a senseless body? . . .

I contain a lesser being which I must obey or suffer an unknown penalty, which is death.

Love and hate are beneath.

Love and hate — *seem* to be accidents.

––––––

Excerpts from M. Teste's Logbook

The unknown that I contain is what makes me myself.

It is the clumsy and uncertain in me that is really me.

My weakness, my frailty. . . .

Lapses are my starting point. My impotence is my origin.

My strength comes from you. The movement in me is from my weakness to my strength.

My real want breeds imaginary riches; and I am that symmetry; I am the act that annuls my desires.

In me there is some ability, more or less developed, to consider — and even to need to consider — my tastes and distastes as purely accidental.

If I knew them better, perhaps I should see necessity in them — instead of accident. But to see necessity, makes it distinct again. . . . Whatever constrains me is not me.

———

Give yourself wholly to your best moment, to your finest memory.

It you must recognize as king of time,

Your finest memory,

The condition to which all discipline must lead you back.

It alone can tell you when to despise yourself, when rightly to admire yourself.

Judge everything by It, for It sets up degrees and measure in your development.

And if It is due to some other than yourself — deny this and know it.

Source of rebound, contempt, and purity.

I sacrifice myself, within, to what I would like to be!

———

The idea, the principle, the flash, the first moment of the first condition, the leap, the jump out of series. . . . To others, the preparation and execution. Cast your net here. This is the place in the sea where you will make your catch. Farewell.

———

. . . The old desire (here you are again, old periodic prompter) to rebuild everything, out of pure materials: nothing but definite parts, nothing but designed contacts and contours, nothing but mastered forms, and nothing vague.

———

Meditations on one's descendants and ascendants.

How strange are these echoes of the ONE.

What? This solid ME has parts outside itself! . . .

. . . This way of looking that altogether contains me, that predicts, that prepares in a certain smile all my explicit thought — this inherence of the *Thing* in the wrinkle at the left corner of my mouth, the pressure of the eyelids,

45

Excerpts from M. Teste's Logbook

and the torsion of the eye muscles — this act essential to me, this definition, this peculiar condition — exists on another face, on the face of some dead person, on this one already and that one still — at various ages, times. Of course — these different copies did not feel the same things; their experiences and their knowledges were quite various . . . but — no matter! *They are never mistaken about themselves* — they divine one another.

There is an admirable mathematical kinship among men. What can be said of this thicket of relations and correspondences? (We haven't even half the words the Romans had to talk about them.) What mixtures, what diffusions!

———

I am infinitely aware of *can* and *will*, because I am infinitely aware of the formless, the accidental that surrounds them like water, and tolerates them, tending always to resume its fatal freedom, its indifferent form, its level of equal chance.

GROUP

Others: my caricature, my model, both.

Others: I sacrifice them, rightly, to silence; I burn them under the very nose of my — soul!

And ME! I tear him to pieces and feed him on his own substance, ru-mi-nated over and over, the only food that will make him grow!

———

Others: I love you weak; strong, I adore and drink you; — I prefer you intelligent and passive . . . unless

Monsieur Teste

(a rare thing) and until (perhaps) another *Self-Same* appear
— an exact response. . . .

Meanwhile, what does the rest matter!

————

In what way is this afternoon, this false light,
this today, these known incidents, these papers, this commonplace everything, different from another everything,
from a *day-before-yesterday*? The senses are not subtle enough
to see that changes have taken place. I know it is not the
same day, but all I do is know it.

My senses are not subtle enough to undo this
work, so delicate and profound, which is the past; not subtle
enough for me to tell that this place or this wall is, perhaps,
not identical with what it was the other day.

IF THE SELF COULD SPEAK

What an insult a compliment is! They dare
praise me! Am I not beyond all qualification? That is what
a Self would say, if it *dared!* —

And if the Self could speak (Refrain).

POEM
(*translated from the Self language*)
O Consciousness!
But I recall
I loved you before, so much!
Perhaps I was about to love you,
O Consciousness!
But now I recall, O Consciousness,
That I loved you before in quite another way!

Excerpts from M. Teste's Logbook

You become memory not of others, but of
yourself,
And more and more you resemble no one else.
More otherwise the self-same, and more same
than myself.
O Mine — but not yet wholly ME!

THE RICH IN SPIRIT

This man had such possessions, such perspectives in himself; he was made of so many years of reading, refutations, meditations, inner combinations, observations; of such ramifications, that his responses were hard to predict; that he did not himself know where he would come out, what aspect would finally strike him, what feeling would prevail in him, what detours and what unexpected simplification would occur, what desire would be born, what retort, what sudden lights! . . .

Perhaps he had reached that strange state of being unable to regard his own decision or inner response as anything but an expedient, knowing quite well that the development of his attention would be infinite and that the *idea* of *finishing* no longer has any meaning in a mind that knows itself well enough. He had come to that point of *inner civilization* where consciousness no longer allows an opinion to go unaccompanied by its procession of modalities, and finds repose (if this *is* repose) only in the awareness of its own wonders, its own practices, substitutions, and innumerable precisions.

. . . In his head or behind his closed eyes, curious rotations occurred — changes, so various, so free, and yet so limited — lights, like the windows of a house seen at night when someone is walking through it with a lamp, like distant revelries, or a night fair; but which, if you could approach, might change into railway stations and dancing savages — or frightful misfortunes — or truths and revelations. . . .

. . . As it were the sanctuary and brothel of possibilities.

The habit of meditation made this mind live in the midst, and by means, of rare states; in a perpetual supposition of purely ideal experiences; in the continual use of extreme conditions and critical phases of thought. . . .

As if extreme rarefactions, unknown vacuums, hypothetical temperatures, monstrous pressures and charges, had been his natural resources — as if nothing could be thought in him unless he submitted it, in the act, to the most energetic treatment, searching over the whole domain of his existence.

———

The taste, and sometimes the talent for *transcendence* — I mean here a *real* incoherence, truer than any imagined coherence, with the sense of being what passes *immediately* from one thing to another, the sense of traversing in some manner the most diverse orders — orders of greatness . . . points of view, strange adjustments. . . . And the sudden return to oneself, breaking off at any point; and the bifid vision, the tripod forms of attention, the contact in another world between things separated in *their own*. . . . All this is myself.

———

Despise your thoughts; they pass, as of themselves — and pass again! . . .

Excerpts from M. Teste's Logbook

THE GAME OF EGO
Rules of the game.
The match is won if we find we deserve our own approval.

If the match has been won by calculation, exercise of the will, with thoroughness, and lucidity — the gain is the greatest possible.

THE GLASS MAN
"So direct is my vision, so pure my senses, so clumsily complete my knowledge, and so free, so clear my fancy, and my learning so consummate that I see through myself from the extreme edge of the world down to my unspoken word; and from the formless rising *thing* of desire, along known fibers and through ordered centers, I *follow and am* myself, answer myself, reflect and echo myself, and quiver to infinity in my mirrors — I am glass."

———

My solitude — which is only the lack, for many years now, of *friends* long and deeply seen; lack of close conversations, dialogues without preamble, without delicacy, except the rarest — costs me dear. It is not living to live without objections, without that living resistance, that prey, that other person, adversary, individuated remnant of the world, obstacle and shadow of myself — another self — an irrepressible, rival intelligence — enemy and best friend, hostility that is divine, fatal — intimate.

Divine, for imagine a god who pregnates, penetrates, infinitely dominates, infinitely divines you — his joy in being combated by his creature trying imperceptibly to be, separate. . . . Devours it to let it be born again; both mutual joy and increase.

If we knew, we should not speak — we should not think, we should not speak to one another.

Knowledge is somehow foreign to being — the latter is unaware, questions itself, makes its own answers. . . .

———

What I have suffered most from? Perhaps from the habit of developing the whole of my thought — of going to the very end of myself.

———

I scorn your ideas in order to consider them in all clarity and almost as the futile ornament of my own; and I see them as we see in perfectly clear water, in a glass vase, three or four goldfish swimming around, always making the same, always naïve, discoveries.

———

I am not stupid because every time I think myself stupid, I deny myself — kill myself.

———

Disgusted with being right, with doing what succeeds, with the efficacy of my methods, must try something else.

4 *Letter from a Friend* *

My friend, here I am, far from you. We were just talking, now I am writing to you. That, *if you will*, is a very strange thing.

You will see that I am in a mood to marvel. The return itself, to Paris, after a rather long absence, has seemed to me somehow metaphysical. I do not mean merely the bodily return, the dark sacrifice of a night to noise and jerks. The inert and living body gives itself over to dead and moving bodies to be transported. The train, an express, has a fixed idea which is the City. You are the captive of its ideal, the puppet of its monotonous rage. You are subjected to millions of blows struck off-stage, rhythms

* *Several good heads having agreed, although without material proof, that this letter was written to M. Teste by a friend of his, a writer, it has been thought that it should be included in this collection — which could do without it, just as it could do without the collection. [Valéry's note.]*

and breaks in rhythm, knocks and mechanical groans — all
the mad racket of some unimaginable factory, making speed.
You are giddy with whirling phantoms, visions spilled into
the void, lights snatched away. The metal forged by movement through the dark makes you imagine that brutal,
personal Time is attacking and disintegrating the deep hard
distance. Badgered by harsh treatment, the over-excited
brain, automatically and almost without knowing it, pro-
duces necessarily a whole modern literature. . . .

Sometimes feeling comes to a standstill. All
the jolting leads to nothing. The sum of all movement is
composed of an infinite number of repeats; each instant con-
vinces the next that we'll never arrive. . . .

Perhaps eternity and hell are the naïve ex-
pressions of some inevitable trip?

Nevertheless, after much shaking of our bones
and ideas in the dark, the sun and Paris finally turn up.

But the being of the mind — *the little man
who is in man* — (and who is always present in the rough
image we have of knowledge), meanwhile works his own
change of presence. He does not circulate, like consciousness,
through a phantasmagoria of visions and a tumult of phenomena. He travels according to his nature, and *in his own
nature.* I should greatly esteem myself if I knew how to
imagine his doings. If I knew how to describe them to you,
my esteem for myself would grow endlessly. But there is no
question of that. . . .

I imagine then, as best I can, that our notion
of moving from one place to another is accompanied by a
process of subtle detachment and reattachment, occurring
in some unknown substance essential to us. A deep classifi-

cation is thus transformed. The moment we decide to depart, long before the body sets out, the idea itself that everything around us is going to change, notifies the hidden system in us of a mysterious modification. The feeling that one is going away makes all things, though still tangible, lose their nearness. They are as if stricken in their powers of presence, and some of them grow faint. Just yesterday, you were with me, and yet there was a secret person in me already fully disposed to see you no more for a long time. I could no longer see you in on-coming time, and yet I was holding your hand. For me you were colored with absence, and somehow condemned to have no imminent future. I looked at you close on, but saw you far off. Your very eyes no longer had duration. It seemed that between you and me there were *two distances*, one still imperceptible, the other already immense; and I did not know which one to take for the more real of the two. . . .

During the journey, I observed the alteration of my soul's expectancies. Certain springs seemed to slacken, others to stiffen. Our unconscious anticipations and our eventual surprise exchange their profound places. If I should meet you tomorrow, it would be a great surprise. . . .

Suddenly I felt *in Paris*, some hours before I was there. I was clearly recovering my Parisian spirits, which had been somewhat dissipated in my travels. They had been reduced to memories; now they were again becoming living values and resources to be used at every moment.

What a demon is the demon of abstract analogy! (You know how he torments me sometimes!) He whispered to me that I should compare this indefinable alteration occurring in me to a rather abrupt change in certain mental *probabilities*. Such and such response, such and such movement, such and such contraction of the face, all of which, in Paris, may be the instantaneous effects of our impressions, are no longer so natural when we are alone in the country, or in the society of a fairly remote place. The spontaneous is no longer the same. We are prepared to respond only to what is *probably at hand*.

This could produce curious consequences. A daring physicist who should include the living, and even hearts, in his experiments, might perhaps risk defining separation as a certain inner distribution. . . .

I am very much afraid, dear old friend, that we are made of many things that do not know us. And it is for that reason we do not know ourselves. If there is an infinite number of such things, then all meditation is useless. . . .

So, I felt myself gripped by another scheme of life, and I knew my return as a kind of vision of the world to which I was returning. A city where verbal life is more powerful, more diverse, more active and capricious than in any other, began taking shape in my mind as a sparkling confusion. And the train's harsh murmur added to my image-filled distraction the accompaniment of a beehive's noise.

It seemed to me that we were moving toward a cloud of talk. A thousand glories evolving, a thousand titles of books *per second* appeared and perished away in this swelling nebula. I could not tell whether I was seeing or hearing this mad stir. There were written words that cried out, spoken words that were men, and men that were names. . . . Nowhere on earth, I thought, does language have more frequency, more resonance, less reserve, than right in Paris where the literature, the science, the arts, the politics of a great country are jealously concentrated. The French have piled up all their ideas within the walls of this one city. And here we live in our own fire.

Tell; retell; foretell; contradict; slander. . . . All these verbs together summed up for me the humming of this paradise of the word.

What could be more tiring than to conceive the chaos of a million minds? Each thought in this tumult has its like, its opposite, its antecedent, and its sequel. So many similarities, so much unforeseen, discourage thought.

Can you imagine the incomparable disorder that can be maintained by ten thousand essentially singular beings? Just imagine the *temperature* that can be produced in this one place by such a great number of *prides*, all comparing themselves. Paris contains and combines, and consummates or consumes most of the brilliant failures summoned by destiny to the *delirious professions*. . . . This is the name I give to all those trades whose main tool is one's opinion of oneself, and whose raw material is the opinion others have of you. Those who follow these trades, doomed to be perpetual apprentices, are necessarily forever afflicted with a kind of delusion of grandeur which is ceaselessly crossed and tormented by a kind of delusion of persecution. This population of uniques is ruled by the law of doing what no one has ever done, what no one will ever do. This is at least the law of the *best*, that is to say, of those who have the courage to want, frankly, something absurd. . . . They live for nothing but to have, and make durable, the illusion of being the only one — for superiority is only a solitude situated at the actual limits of a species. Each one founds his existence on the non-existence of others, but from them he must extort their consent not to exist. . . . Please notice that I am only deducing what is contained in what is seen. If you doubt, just ask yourself where an effort leads to, which absolutely cannot be made but by one particular individual, and which depends on the particularity of men? Think of the real meaning of a hierarchy founded on rarity. I sometimes like to apply an image, taken from physics, to our hearts, intimately composed as they are of an enormous amount of injustice and a bit of justice, in combination. I imagine in each of us an atom more important than the others, and composed of two *grains of energy* wanting to be separated. These energies are contradictory but indivisible. Nature has joined them forever, although they are furious enemies. One is the eternal movement of a large *positive electron*, and this movement generates a series of grave sounds which the inner ear, with no trouble at all, makes out to be a deep monotonous phrase: *There's only me. There's only me. There's only me, me, me.* . . . As for the small, radically *negative* electron, it screams at the extreme pitch of shrillness, piercing again and again in the cruelest fashion the other's egotistical theme: *Yes, but there is so-and-so. . . . Yes, but there is so-and-so. . . . And so-and-so, and so-and-so!* For the name changes, often. . . .

A bizarre kingdom where all the beautiful things growing there are bitter food for all souls but one. And the more beautiful they are, the bitterer their taste.

Or again. It seems to me that every mortal possesses, very nearly at the center of his mechanism, and well placed among the instruments for navigating his life, a tiny apparatus of incredible sensitivity which indicates the state of his self-respect. There we read whether we admire ourselves, adore ourselves, despise ourselves, or should blot ourselves out; and some living pointer, trembling over the secret dial, flickers with terrible nimbleness between the zero of a beast and the maximum of a god.

Now, my kind friend, if you want to understand something about a good many things, just imagine that so vital and so delicate an apparatus is a plaything for anyone that comes along.

And, no doubt, there are strange men in whom this hidden needle always indicates the point opposite the one you might suppose. They hate themselves at the very moment they are universally esteemed, and contrariwise in the contrary case. But we know that laws are no longer completely fulfilled. Now there are only the nearly so.

And the train was still running, violently flinging back poplars, cows, barns, and all earthly things, as if it thirsted, as if it were rushing toward pure thought, or to catch some star. What supreme goal can exact such brutal ravishment, and such swift consignment of countryside to the devil?

We were approaching the cloud. Several names grew luminous. The sky was filled with political and literary meteors. Surprises were crackling. The gentle were bleating, the bitter were caterwauling, the fat were bellowing, the thin were screaming.

Parties, schools, salons, cafés were all making themselves heard. Air no longer sufficing, the ether was being charged with messages. I was deafened by the clashes of a duel in which the swords were flashes of lightning, and poverties were multiplied to the ends of the world with the speed of light.

I beg you to excuse me for my abuse here of the imperfect of the indicative, but it is the tense of incoherence; and I perceive that I am in the act of painting, if this *is* painting, the greatest incoherence conceivable. I shall add several strokes to it by using a few other *imperfects*.

I was seeing in my mind the market, the stock exchange, the Occidental bazaars for the exchange of phantasms. I was occupied with the wonders of the transitory, and its astonishing duration, with the force of paradox, with the resistance of worn-out things. . . . Everything appeared in images. Abstract struggles took the form of a sorcery of devils. Fashion and eternity collared each other. The retrograde and the advanced were contesting at what point to occur. Novelties, even new ones, were giving birth to very old consequences. What silence had elaborated was cried for sale. . . . In short, all possible spiritual events passed rapidly before my soul, that was still half asleep. Still limp and confused, it was seized with terror, disgust, despair, and frightful curiosity, contemplating the ideal spectacle of this immense activity called intellectual. . . .

———

INTELLECTUAL?

This enormous word, coming vaguely upon me, sharply *blocked* my whole train of visions. How curious is the shock of a word in a head! The whole mass of the *false*, at full speed, suddenly jumps out of line with the *true*. . . .

Intellectual? . . . No answer. No ideas. Trees, signal disks, harps without number, from the horizontal strings of which, plains, châteaux, and wisps of smoke, fluttered out. . . . I was now looking into myself with foreign eyes, stumbling about in what I had just created. Bewildered in the midst of this débris of the intelligible, I found, lying inert and as if knocked down, the big word that had caused the catastrophe. It was no doubt a little too long for the curves of my thought.

Intellectual. . . . Anyone in my place would have understood. But me! . . .

You know, dear You, that my mind is of the most shadowy kind. You know by experience, and better still for having heard it said a hundred times. There are plenty of people, learned, and benign, and well disposed, who are waiting until I am translated into French, to read me. They complain of me to the public, they expose before it citations of my verse which I confess must perplex them. They even take a righteous pride in not understanding something; a fact others might hide. — "*Modeste tamen et circumspecto judicio pronuntiandum est,*" said Quintilian, in a passage that Racine has taken care to translate, "*ne quod plerisque accidit, damnent quæ non intelligunt.*" But for my part I am extremely sorry to grieve these lovers of light. Nothing really attracts me but clarity. But alas, friend of mine! I assure you that I find almost none at all. I whisper this close into your ear; do not spread it about. Guard my secret excessively. Yes, for me clarity is so uncommon that over the whole extent of the world — and particularly of the thinking and writing world — I see it only in the proportion of diamond to the mass of the planet. The darkness people find in me is vain and transparent beside that I discover almost everywhere. Happy are those who agree among themselves that they understand one another perfectly! They write or speak without trembling. You can sense how much I envy all those lucid beings, whose works make us dream of the sweet facility of the sun in a crystal universe. . . . My bad conscience suggests sometimes that I should defend myself by accusing them. It whispers to me that only those who seek nothing never run into obscurity, and that we should suggest to people only what they know already. But I look into my own depths, and I am forced to agree with what so many distinguished persons say. It is true, my friend, I have an unfortunate mind, one that is never quite sure it understands what it has understood without realizing it. I have great difficulty in distinguishing what is clear without reflection from what is positively obscure. . . . This failing is no doubt the principle of my darkness. I distrust all words, for the least meditation shows that it is absurd to trust them. I have reached the point, alas, of comparing those words on which we so lightly traverse the space of a thought, to light planks thrown across an abyss, which permit crossing but no stopping. A man in quick motion can use them and get away; but if he hesitates the least bit in the world, this fraction of time breaks them down, and all together fall into the depths. The one who hurries is *clever;* he must not dwell heavily: he would soon find the clearest speech to be a tissue of obscure terms.

All this might very well lead me into a long and charming inquiry, which I spare you. A letter is literature. There is a strict law in literature that we must never go to the bottom of anything. This is also the general will. Just look around, everywhere.

So, I was in my own abyss — which for being

Letter from a Friend

my own was no less an abyss — so I was in my own abyss, unable to explain to a child, to a savage, to an archangel — to myself, this word, *Intellectual*, which gives nobody else any difficulty at all.

It wasn't that images failed me. On the contrary, every time this terrible word consulted my mind, the oracle responded with a different image. All were naïve. Not one of them precisely annulled the sensation of not understanding.

Tatters of dream came to me.

I formed figures which I called "Intellectuals." Men almost motionless, who caused great movement in the world. Or very animated men, by the lively action of whose hands and mouths, imperceptible powers and essentially invisible objects were made manifest. . . . Pardon me for telling you the truth. I saw what I saw.

Men of *thought*, Men of *letters*, Men of *science*, *Artists* — Causes, living causes, individuate causes, minimal causes, causes within causes and inexplicable to themselves — and causes whose effects were as vain, but at the same time as prodigiously important, *as I wished*. . . . The universe of these causes and their effects existed and did not exist. This system of strange acts, productions, and prodigies had the all-powerful and vacant reality of a game of cards. Inspirations, meditations, works, glory, talents, it took no more than a certain look to make these things nearly everything, and a certain other look to reduce them to nearly nothing.

Then, in an apocalyptic flash, I seemed to glimpse the disorder and ferment of a whole society of demons. There appeared, in some supernatural space, a sort of comedy of what happens in History. Struggles, factions, triumphs, solemn execrations, executions, riots, tragedies over power! In this Republic all rumors were of scandal, of colossal or collapsing fortunes, of plots and assaults. There were committee-room plebiscites, insignificant coronations, many assassinations *by word*. I do not even mention the pilfering. This whole population of "intellectuals" was like the other. Among them were puritans, speculators, prostitutes, believers who seemed to be infidels and infidels who put on the face of believers; some posed as fools, some were fools; there were authorities, and anarchists, and even executioners whose blades inspired disgust for ink. Some believed themselves priests and pontiffs, others prophets, still others Cæsars, or even martyrs, or a little of each. Several, even in their acts, took themselves for children or women. The most ridiculous were those who made themselves, on their own authority, the judges and justices of the tribe. They did not seem in the least to suspect that our judgments judge us, and that nothing reveals us, exposes our weaknesses more ingenuously than the attitude of pronouncing upon our fellows. It is a dangerous art, one in which the slightest errors may always be attributed to our character.

Each of these demons looked at himself rather frequently in a paper mirror; there, he saw the highest or lowest of beings. . . .

I was vaguely seeking the laws of this empire. The necessity to amuse; the need to live; the desire to survive; the pleasure of surprising, shocking, rebuking, teaching, despising; the needle of jealousy, all drove, irritated, excited, and explained this Hell.

Letter from a Friend

I saw myself there also; and under a guise unknown to me, which my writings, perhaps, had formed. You are not unaware, dear dreamer, that in dreams a *singular* accord sometimes occurs between what we see and what we know; but it is not an accord that would be borne out in waking. I *see* Peter, and I *know* it is James. So, I perceived myself, though rarely, and with another face; I recognized myself only by an exquisite pain that pierced my heart. It seemed to me that one of us, the phantom or I, must *faint away. . . .*

Good-by. I should never have done if I tried to note for you all that took color to confound me in the final moments of my journey. Good-by. I was about to forget to tell you that I was roused out of all this by the foot of a crusty Englishman, which crushed mine with no trouble at all, just as the black sweating train came to a stop. Good-by.

Paul Valéry had, before his death, set aside a number of notes and sketches, intending to use them for a new edition of Monsieur Teste.

The fragments that follow, dating from various periods of his life, have been selected from that number.

5

A walk with M. Teste

   I sometimes meet myself, on summer morn-
ings about eleven o'clock, among idlers on a sidewalk not far
from the Madeleine where I usually go, to stroll, smoke, and
reflect on what the day's paper says, or rather to think over
all it does not say. Before long, I run into M. Teste meditat-
ing in the opposite direction along the same easy line.

   We each give up our separate ideas, and, together, watch the mild and incomprehensible flow of the
street, bearing along shadows, circles, fluid constructions,
slight acts, and now and then bringing us some purer and
exquisite one: a being, an eye, or some delicate animal making
a thousand golden forms and playing with the ground.

   We drink the delicious passage. We watch the
dappled light making everybody haphazardly smile, flitting
over the forehead of a hurrying woman who glides and

threads her way among the slender cars, and among other events. The pale buildings are a headland of soft shadow with velvet balconies, hanging abrupt there against a sky barely downed with light; and in front of us, drowned in the pure immensity of daylight reflected from the ground, passers have come, are like us, and will separate into the sun.

We listen with delicate ear to the mixture of noises in the ample street; our heads are filled with abounding nuances of the footstep of tufted horses and interminable man, vaguely animating the distance with a rumble as in a dream, a kind of confused beat that trembles and is composed of walking, the opulent molting of the world, the transformation of undistinguished persons into one another, the general press of the crowd.

We are silent, and look at each other, anxious not to be a fragment of the crowd. But as for me, the enormous *other* presses in on me from all sides. It does my breathing for me in its own impenetrable substance. If I smile, a bit of its enchanted pulp, not far from my mind, wrinkles; and, with this change in my lips, I suddenly feel subtle.

I do not know what is my own: I am not even sure of this smile, nor its consequence which is half thought.

Whatever makes me unique is mixed with the vast body and passing plenty of this place; over there, people, the grist of politics, flow among a few persons, and across my reflections a flame of air and men, endlessly reproducing itself, blows, wavers, anticipates, and sometimes precisely constitutes my thought.

A continual power of beginning and ending

consumes these beings, parts of beings, doubts, walking phrases, girls; endless colors like a fine horse bearing the whole scene away, even those moments that vanish in a peculiar void. . . .

Dialogue

Man is different from me, from you. That which thinks is never that which it thinks about, and since the first is a form with a voice, the second takes all forms and all voices. So, no one is man, M. Teste least of all.

Neither was he a philosopher, nor anything of that kind, nor even a *littérateur;* that is why he did a great deal of thinking — for the more we write, the less we think.

He was always adding to something, I do not know what: perhaps he was constantly quickening his manner of conceiving: perhaps he was enjoying the abundant resources of solitary thinking. Whether one or the other, he remains the most satisfactory being I have met — that is, the only individual who endures in my mind.

Consequently, he was neither good, nor mean, nor fake, nor cynical, nor anything else; all he did was choose: which is the power to make a pleasing combination out of a moment and oneself.

He had one advantage over everyone else, which he had created: that is, he had a handy idea of himself; and into each of his thoughts went another M. Teste, a character he knew well, simplified, and joined to the true at every point . . . in short he had substituted for the vague notion of ourselves which alters all our calculations and slyly involves us in our own speculations (thus falsifying them) a definite imaginary being, a Self, well trained, or bred, true as an instrument, sensitive as an animal, and compatible with everything, like man.

So, armed with his own image, Teste at every moment knew his own weakness and his own strength. For him, the world was composed, first of what he knew and what he possessed, all of which no longer counted; second, in another self, of all the rest; which might or might not be acquired, constructed, transformed. He wasted his time neither with the impossible nor with the easy.

One evening he replied to me: "The infinite, my friend, no longer amounts to much — just a trick of the pen. *The universe exists only on paper.*

"No idea can represent it. None of the senses lead to it. You can say it, and that is all."

"But science," I said, "uses . . ."

"Science! There are only scientists, my friend, scientists and their good days. They are men . . . feeling

Dialogue

their way; they have bad nights, or a sour stomach, or an excellent lucid afternoon. Do you know what the first hypothesis of all science is, the idea no scientist can do without? It is this: *the world is not known.* Yes, exactly. Now, we often think the opposite; there are moments when everything seems clear, fulfilled, and there are no problems. At such times, science no longer exists — or, if you will, science is complete. But at other times, nothing is evident; there are only gaps, acts of faith, uncertainty; we see nothing but scraps and irreducible objects, everywhere.

"Since all this is more or less recognized, we must now find out how to go back, without fail, from the second condition to the first, how to transform at will the anxious mind of the moment into the tranquil possessor of a moment ago. But there is a touch of madness in the desire to do this."

"Well and good," I replied. "Yet, in every imaginable case, you will admit, being is still strange. To be in some particular way, is stranger still. It is even a bother."

And I added, repeating what occurs to everyone who is a bit simple:

"After all, what am I doing here?"

"So," said M. Teste, "you want to know what you are doing here. . . ."

"And yet, why? The really odd thing is that I should wonder. Why do I want to know . . ."

"Because you have thought about it."

"You are making fun of me, you are pulling my leg."

"Doubtless," said M. Teste.

"Let's come back," I said, "to human destiny." (And I had hardly spoken when I felt myself turn silly.)

"I wonder," M. Teste thought out loud, "what it is about man's 'destiny' (as you say) that interests me. About as much as . . . the goddess Barbara — who has never been heard of, and I suddenly invent her name. It is the same thing exactly! Is it because, at bottom, people are stirred by nothing but the absurd? That is one thing I have no use for."

"Neither have other really superior men," I said, trying to save myself.

"Simpleton," cried M. Teste, "don't compare me with others: in the first place, you don't know me; and in the next, you don't know others."

"As for that stupid lightning called enthusiasm, learn to bottle it, or put it on conducting wires. *Distinguish it* from the foolish objects for which people generally feel it, in which they put it. Foolish because these objects are this or that, and not what you choose. Burn, brilliantly, but only at your own command; scorn particulars, and draw power from everything. Yet, a thousand things are constantly null, if you will. Their nothingness is at your disposition. . . . For example, the stupid always boast of their humanity, the weak of their sense of justice; confusion is to the interest of both parties. Let's avoid the herd, and keep out of the scales of such ignorant Justice; let's fight those who want to make us like themselves. Remember, quite simply, that between men there can exist only two relations: logic and war. Always demand proof, proof is the fundamental respect you owe yourself. If they refuse, remember that you are being attacked and that every means will be used to make you

Dialogue

obey. You will be taken in by the sweetness or charm of no matter what, you will be passionate with somebody else's passion; you will be made to think what you have neither considered nor weighed; you will be overtaken with tenderness, delight, ecstasy; you will draw conclusions from premises that have been fabricated for you, and you will, with considerable ingenuity, relearn . . . everything you already know by heart."

"The difficulty is to see what is," I sighed.

"Yes," said M. Teste, "that is, not to confuse words. We must realize that we can arrange them as we will, and that for every combination we make, there does not necessarily exist some other corresponding thing. There are at least two hundred words we must forget, and when we hear them, translate them. For instance, the word 'Right' should be blotted out of our minds, and everywhere else, so no one will be fooled by it."

"That is hard," I replied, "it hurts. No more error, and I like error."

And so we went, on and on.

7

For a Portrait of M. Teste

GENTLEMEN: The term *aberration* is quite often taken in a bad sense, to mean a departure from the normal for the worse, a symptom of deterioration and decay in the mental faculties, manifested either by perversions of taste, delirious speech, or strange, sometimes lawless behavior. But in certain branches of science, this same word, although retaining a certain pathological coloring, may designate some excess of vitality, a kind of overflow of internal energy, resulting in an abnormally high production of organs or physical or psychical activity. It is in this sense that botany speaks of aberrant vegetation, and that, in a certain sense, most of the vegetable species that man uses for his own needs, like grain, the vine, the rose, etc. . . . ., are products of immemorial methods of culture which have produced varieties that one may call aberrant, despite their utility or their beauty. We have thought it well to preface with the fore-going remarks this review of an unusual case, well known in the world of psychology as the "case of M. Teste."

———

M. Teste was born of chance. Like everybody else. All the mind he has or had comes from this fact.

———

There is no sure likeness of M. Teste.
Every portrait of him differs from the others.
The man with no reflection:
The ghost who is our *self* — which he *feels he is* — and who is clothed with *our* weight.
Just imagine the meaning of the words: My weight!
What a possessive! . . .

How can weight be distinguished from the energy that makes it what it is — heavy, light, etc. . . .

———

M. Teste is *the witness.*

That in us which is the production of *all* and therefore nothing — reaction itself, withdrawal into the self.
Imagine the eye — the seeing as opposed to the seen. The seen is paid for by that which destroys it to preserve the faculty of seeing, and can exist only by *using up the possible* and recharging.

For a Portrait of M. Teste

Now, imagine a man who should be, as it were, the allegory and hero of this process.

Conscious — Teste, *Testis*.
Imagine an "eternal" observer whose role is nothing more than to rehearse and demonstrate the system whose *Self* is that instantaneous part that thinks it is the Whole.
The Self could never manage to function if it did not believe . . . it was all.

All at once the *suavis mamilla* he is touching becomes a thing restricted to what it is.
The sun itself. . . .
The "nonsense" of everything is suddenly apparent. Nonsense, that is particularity as opposed to generality. "Smaller than" becomes the terrible sign of the mind. The Demon of prearranged possibilities.

———

Man observed, watched, spied upon by his "ideas," by memory.

———

The most complete psychic transformer, no doubt, that ever was.
The reverse of a madman (*aberration*, which is so important in nature, in him is conscious) for he always returned to himself richer no doubt; able to carry dissociations, substitutions, similitudes to their extreme because he was sure of his return, an infallible reverse operation.

Monsieur Teste

Everything seemed to him a particular case of the functioning of his mind, a functioning that itself had become conscious, identical with the sense or idea he had of it.

At the end of the mind, the body. But at the end of the body, the mind.

Pain tried to invent a mechanism that would convert pain into knowledge — a process that mystics have glimpsed, vaguely. But the reverse was the beginning of this experiment.

God is not far. He is what is closest.

————

In Teste, the psychic function occurs at the peak of separation of inner changes and *values*.

Thought is likewise distinct (when he is HIM-SELF) from its similarities and confusions with the *World*, and, on the other hand, from affective values. He contemplates it in its state of pure chance.

Or rather he is himself a reaction to such a scene, which requires to be witnessed by Someone.

The notion of external things is a restriction upon inner combinations.

Significant imagination is a kind of affective trickery.

How to come back from so far?

————

Jealous of his best ideas, of those he thinks his best, sometimes so personal, so much his own that their

For a Portrait of M. Teste

expression in common unprivate language can only give, outwardly, the feeblest and falsest notion of them. And who knows but what those ideas that are most important in governing a mind are not as peculiar to it, as strictly personal as clothes, or an article adapted to the body? Who knows whether one's real "philosophy" is . . . communicable?

So, T. was jealous of his separate clarities. He thought: What is an idea if it is not endowed with the value of a State secret, or a secret of art? . . . if we are not ashamed of it, as if it were a sin or a disease? Hide your god — Hide your devil.

In plays, we put a peculiar value on ourselves, whether we take part in person or remain a hidden presence.

And yet, how do we choose a character to be ourselves, how exactly does our center take shape?

Why, in the theater of the mind, are you You? — *You* and not *Me*?

So, this mechanism is not the most general one possible.

If it were . . . there would be no more *absolute me*.

But isn't that just what M. Teste is seeking: to withdraw from the self, the ordinary self, by constantly trying to diminish, to combat, to compensate for the irregularity, the anisotropy of consciousness.

———

M. Teste comes in — and everyone present is struck by his "simplicity."

He looks absolute — his face and gesture are
of an indefinable *simplicity*.

Etc. . . .

He is one who thinks (from long training,
from habit become nature) continually and on every occasion according to data and studied definitions. Everything
is referred to himself, and, in himself, to strict rules. Man of
precision — and living distinctions.

———

In this strange man, the keenest and clearest
act of memory existed as a *present* event in his mind, and
even the sense of the *past* in a particular image was accompanied by the notion that the *past* is a fact of the *present* —
a sort of . . . *color* of some image — or perhaps it is prompt-
ness in precise and exact response.

———

Up to a fairly mature age, M. Teste was not
in the least aware that his mind was *unusual*. He believed
everyone else was like himself, but thought himself more
foolish and worthless than most. This observation led him
to take note of his failures, and sometimes his successes.
He noticed that quite often he was better than the best and
worse than the worst; a dangerous observation since it may
lead to a policy of abuse and oddly made concessions.

———

Recollections of M. Teste — *Diary of Teste's
Friend.*

For a Portrait of M. Teste

One of Teste's pet notions, and not his least fanciful, was wanting to keep art — *Ars* — and yet do away with the artist's or author's illusions. He couldn't bear the stupid pretensions of poets — the gross pretensions of novelists. He insisted that a clear idea of what you are doing will give much more surprising and universal results than all the nonsense about inspiration, characters *true to life*, etc. . . . If Bach had believed the spheres were dictating his music, he would not have had the power of limpidity and the sovereign control of transparent combinations that he had. Staccato.

(November 34)

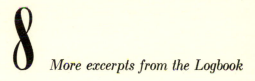

8
More excerpts from the Logbook

One should go into himself armed to the teeth.

———

Make a "proprietor's" tour of inspection in oneself.

State of being in anyone who has done with abstract words — who has broken with them.

———

Create a kind of anguish in order to resolve it.

———

The game played with oneself.

The effect on others must never forget their

Monsieur Teste

mechanics — quantities, intensities, potentials — and treat them not only as *themselves*, but as machines, and animals — whence an *art*.

———

"A very old remark of mine which I have a weakness for is that the shorter the interval of time at which men are observed the more alike they are, so that they are indistinguishable in a *single instant*. Another, no less dear to my mind, is that this very similarity among men, increasing toward identity, is a result of the intensity of their emotions."

(Cf. M. Teste). *It is natural* to want to know whether these two factors of (neuro-psychic) identity could not perhaps be joined.

In fact, haste will do it, or surprise, etc.

So, there are conditions to the limits.

———

"At the bottom of thought are crossroads."

"I am the unstable."

"The mind is possibility at its maximum, the maximum capacity for incoherence."

"The SELF is the instantaneous reaction to each partial incoherence, which is a *stimulus*."

———

I wish to borrow from the (visible) world only forces — not forms, but that which makes forms.

Not history, not decoration and scenery, but

More excerpts from the Logbook

the feel of matter itself, rock, air, water, vegetation — and their elemental powers.

And acts and phases — not individuals and their memory.

———

The first thing is to go over your domain.

Then put a fence around it, for although it is bounded by other external circumstances, you still want to count for something in setting bounds you did not create.

Man tries to will what he did not will.

He is given a prison, and says: I am locking myself up.

He cannot any more get out of it than a man can get out of a dungeon by counting its stones — any more than phrases scribbled on the walls can make them fall.

———

No one would think of *explaining movement* by considerations of *color*, whereas the contrary is, or has been, attempted. So, it doesn't work both ways. Perhaps it is because we are sources of movement but not of color — and this power is the condition of our explanation.

I say: sources. But in the sense that we are sources of pain or sensual pleasure. We feel "coming from *ourselves*" certain . . . (how shall I say?) modifications — certain values — grandeurs, "sensations" — certain "accel-erations" which are at once most *ours* and most strange, our masters, our *selves* of the moment, and the *coming moment*.

How can depths so variable and referenceless be described, depths which have the most important but most unstable bearing on "thought"? Music alone can do it. A kind of *field* that dominates the phenomena of consciousness — images, ideas, which without it would only be *combinations*, a symmetrical arrangement of combinations.

Cf. M. Teste — the epic difference between the *objectivity* that makes combinations and the *field* in question.

———

The mind must not be concerned with persons:

De personis non curandum.

———

The thing that is really important to one — I mean the one in us who is in essence unique and alone — is just that which makes him feel that he is alone.

This is clear to him when he is *really alone* (even while materially with others.)

———

Emotions to be considered as nonsense, weakness, vanity, stupidity, imperfection — humiliating, like seasickness and fear of high places.

. . . Something in us, or in me, revolts against the soul's inventive power over the mind.

———

. . . At times, SOMEONE who is a complete

stranger to the body and the sensibility speaks our words, in *his own* interests.

He sees and coldly describes life, death, danger, passion, everything in us that is human — but as someone else, a witness who is all mind. . . .

Is it the soul?

No. For this someone is, as it were, beyond all "affectivity." He is pure knowledge, with a peculiar detachment and disregard for the rest — like an eye that could see what it sees without giving any but chromatic value. . . . This *someone* would count the buttons on the hangman's coat. . . .

————

I despise what I know — what I can do.

What I can do has the same weakness or strength as my body. My "soul" begins at the very point where I can see no further, where I can do nothing more — where my mind closes its own road ahead — and coming back from the greater depths, looks condescendingly at the mark on the sounding-line, at the catch in the net, a sorry haul brought up from the middling deeps. . . . Why so much trouble, so much joy over such a take? Which is the more ridiculous, to be ashamed or to rejoice over the answer we give ourselves?

————

Man's only hope is to discover means of action which will diminish his evil and increase his good, that is, something which can directly or indirectly furnish his sensibility with the means of acting upon itself, by its own laws.

Give an account, here, of what has been done in this direction. The sensibility is everything, supports everything, evaluates everything.

———

"Ideas," for me, are means of transformation — consequently they are phases or moments of some change.
      An "idea" of man "is a means of transforming a question."

———

      Myself, you are full of secrets which you call Me.

You are the voice of the unknown in you.

———

I feel no need for anyone else's feelings, and I take no pleasure in affecting them. My own are enough. Intrigues, however, may divert me, provided I do not see that I may easily alter them.

———

I need nothing. And even the word "need" has no meaning for me. So this is what I am going to do. I shall give myself an aim; and yet nothing is outside of me. I shall even make some beings that resemble me a bit, and I shall give them eyes and reason. I shall also give them a very vague suspicion of my existence, so they will be led, by the very reason I have endowed them with, to deny my existence; and their eyes shall be so made that they can see an infinite number of things but not me.

More excerpts from the Logbook

This done, I shall impose on them the need to imagine me, see me despite their eyes, and define me despite their reason.

And I shall be the answer to the riddle. I shall reveal myself to those who solve this puzzle-universe and who are contemptuous enough of the organs and means I have invented, to conclude against their evidence and their clear thought.

———

I do not face the world, I face the WALL. There's not the least speck on the wall I do not know.

For me, he said, the most violent feelings have something else in them — a sign — that tells me to despise them. It is simply that I *feel* them coming from beyond my kingdom, once I have wept, or laughed.

———

Pain occurs when consciousness resists some local change in the body. A pain that we could clearly conceive and, as it were, circumscribe would become sensation without suffering — in this way, we might perhaps come to know something directly about the depths of our body — a knowledge of the same order as that we find in music. Pain is musical, we can almost speak of it in musical terms. There are sharps and flats, andantes and furiosos, sustained notes, rests, arpeggios, progressions — sudden silences, etc.

———

"Well" (says M. Teste). "The essential is against life."

———

Liberty — Generality

All I do and think is only a Sample of my possibilities.

Man is more — more general — than his life and acts. He is somehow *made* for more eventualities than he can know.

M. Teste says: My possibilities never leave me.

———

And the Dæmon says to him: Give me proof. Show me that you *still are* the one you thought you were.

9

End of M. Teste

It is a matter of going from zero to zero. And that is life. From the unconscious and senseless to the unconscious and senseless.

Impossible to see the passage, since it goes from seeing to not seeing, after first going from not seeing to seeing. Seeing is not being, not exactly; seeing implies being. One can be without seeing, which means that seeing may be cut off. We become aware of its stopping by the changes that come over us . . . which are revealed by a kind of seeing called memory. The difference between "present" seeing and "past" seeing, or memory, if there is a break between them, and if present seeing does not contain the other, may be attributed to intervening "time." This hypothesis has never been found at fault.

The strange look at things, the look of a man

who does *not recognize*, who is not of this world, the eye that
is a frontier between being and not-being — belongs to the
thinker. It is also the look of a dying man, of a man losing
recognition. Thus it is optional: the thinker is either a dying
man, or a Lazarus. Perhaps not so optional.

M. Teste said to me:

Good-by. Soon . . . the end . . . of a certain
way of seeing. Perhaps suddenly and now. Perhaps tonight,
a decline that little by little will become unaware even of
itself. Yet, I have worked all my life toward this minute.

After a while, before the finish, perhaps, I
shall have that important moment — perhaps I shall be-
hold the entire sum of myself in one terrible flash. . . . Not
possible.

Syllogisms debased by agony, thousands of
joyful images bathed in pain, fear joined to fine moments of
the past.

And yet, what a temptation death is.

An unimaginable thing that enters the mind
in forms of desire and horror, turnabout.

Intellectual end. Funeral march of thought.

COLOPHON

*Typography and binding design by
Alvin Lustig. The book is set in Monotype
Bodoni, which catches more accurately than
most cuttings the spirit of the original
Bodoni type.
Composition, printing, and binding by
The Plimpton Press, Norwood, Mass.*